KU-223-811

HER SHEIKH BOSS

BY
CAROL GRACE

North Lanarkshire Council
Motherwell Library
Hamilton Road, Motherwell
MOB3

7 775110 40	
Askews	09-May-2008
	£2.99

®MILLS & BOON®
Pure reading pleasure

DID YOU PURCHASE THIS BOOK WITHOUT A COVER?

If you did, you should be aware it is **stolen property** as it was reported *unsold and destroyed* by a retailer. Neither the author nor the publisher has received any payment for this book.

All the characters in this book have no existence outside the imagination of the author, and have no relation whatsoever to anyone bearing the same name or names. They are not even distantly inspired by any individual known or unknown to the author, and all the incidents are pure invention.

All Rights Reserved including the right of reproduction in whole or in part in any form. This edition is published by arrangement with Harlequin Enterprises II BV/S.à.r.l. The text of this publication or any part thereof may not be reproduced or transmitted in any form or by any means, electronic or mechanical, including photocopying, recording, storage in an information retrieval system, or otherwise, without the written permission of the publisher.

This book is sold subject to the condition that it shall not, by way of trade or otherwise, be lent, resold, hired out or otherwise circulated without the prior consent of the publisher in any form of binding or cover other than that in which it is published and without a similar condition including this condition being imposed on the subsequent purchaser.

® and TM are trademarks owned and used by the trademark owner and/or its licensee. Trademarks marked with ® are registered with the United Kingdom Patent Office and/or the Office for Harmonisation in the Internal Market and in other countries.

First published in Great Britain 2008
Harlequin Mills & Boon Limited,
Eton House, 18-24 Paradise Road, Richmond, Surrey TW9 1SR

© Carol Culver 2008

ISBN: 978 0 263 86514 1

Set in Times Roman 13 on 14¾ pt
02-0508-50650

Printed and bound in Spain
by Litografia Rosés, S.A., Barcelona

Carol Grace has always been interested in travel and living abroad. She spent her junior year in college at the Sorbonne, and later toured the world on the hospital ship *HOPE*. She and her husband have lived and worked in Iran and Algeria. Carol says writing is another way of making her life exciting. Her office is her mountain-top home overlooking the Pacific Ocean, which she shares with her inventor husband. Her daughter is a lawyer and her son is an actor/writer. She's written thirty books for Silhouette, and she also writes single titles. She's thrilled to be writing for Mills & Boon® Romance. Check out her website— carolgracebooks.com—to find out more about Carol's books. Come and blog with her fun-loving fellow authors at fogcitydivas.com

DESERT BRIDES

When an ordinary girl meets a sheikh…

*If you love reading stories set in distant, exotic lands
where women just like you are swept off their feet
by mysterious, gorgeous desert princes—
then you'll love this mini-series!*

*Look out for more **Desert Brides** stories
coming soon from Mills & Boon® Romance.*

In July, Nicola Marsh sweeps you away to
an exotic desert with a breathtaking man in
The Desert Prince's Proposal.

Enjoy!

CHAPTER ONE

"GOOD news."

Claudia looked up from her desk to see her boss, Sheikh Samir Al-Hamri standing in the doorway to her office, his arms folded over his chest, a smile on his devastatingly handsome face.

"The merger's going through?" They'd been working out a deal for months with a rival shipping company in his country of Tazzatine.

"Finally. It's been a long road and I couldn't have done it without you."

Claudia blushed at the compliment. She knew he appreciated her input, her willingness to work long hours and her devotion to the job. What he wouldn't appreciate, if he knew about it, was her devotion to him personally. She tried, heaven knows she tried to treat him like any other boss, but how could she when he wasn't like any other boss?

He was a sheikh, a member of the ruling family in his country, with more money than anyone could spend in a lifetime, dazzling good looks, the best education in the world and even a sense of humor. And generous. How could she forget generous, when he gave her large raises without her asking? The one thing he wasn't generous about was vacations. He didn't take them and he didn't see why she should, either.

Claudia didn't care. If she was on vacation, she wouldn't get to see him every day. Wouldn't get to discuss new shipping routes, the GNP of developing countries, or fluctuating petroleum prices. Who else would want to talk about alternate sources of energy or the future of container ships? Nobody in her knitting group or her book club. But who would have thought these subjects would interest a twenty-eight-year-old former English major like Claudia?

When she first took the job it was just a job. High-paying, demanding and high-energy. But working for Samir had been an eye-opener. His enthusiasm for the field of international shipping, the field he'd been born into and raised to inherit, was contagious. Now she took a real interest in the workings and the future of his family's business.

"Your family must be pleased," she said.

He hesitated a moment then walked to the window of her office and looked out across San Francisco Bay sparkling in the morning sunlight to Alcatraz, Angel Island and the Golden Gate Bridge.

"They are," he said. "Very pleased. It's the end of an era, the end to hostility and competition between the Al-Hamris and the Bayadhis, but…"

She waited for him to finish his sentence. He didn't. Something was wrong. She knew him so well, knew he should be on the phone, calling friends, making plans, sharing the news with everyone including the press. Instead he was just standing there lost in thought.

"What about the papers?" She held up the file with the contract in it. "Nothing's been signed yet." Maybe that was it. He was afraid to count on the deal until it was official.

"That will happen in Tazzatine in our home office on the twenty-first of this month." He looked over at the photograph of the high-rise, waterfront headquarters of the Al-Hamri Shipping Company surrounded by residence towers, a sports complex and a shopping plaza. "For now, they have our word, we have theirs."

"You should be celebrating. Should I book a table at La Grenouille for tonight?"

He turned to face her. He rubbed his hand over his brow and didn't speak for a long moment. "Sure," he said finally. "Why not? And get two first class tickets to Tazzatine on…" He crossed the room to look at the calendar on the wall. "Say, the fifteenth. Leave the return open."

Claudia scribbled the date on her notepad. "Two?"

"Two. You and I."

Her mouth fell open. "I'm going with you?" She'd never gone anywhere further than an hour or two away to meetings in Silicon Valley or Sacramento with him in the two years she'd worked there. Now she was going halfway around the world? "You're not serious."

"Of course I am. You're the one who wrote up the proposal in the first place. You have the details of the contract in your head. You don't think I'd sign anything without your being there, do you?"

"I…uh…"

"Especially something this important. Who knows what could go wrong at the last minute? Changes to be made? Objections? I need you there. You know I'm no good at details."

He was right. He was the one with the big plans, the overview. He was the rainmaker. She took care of the details. They were a team.

"I think I should stay here in the office. If you need me, you can always call me," she said.

"No good. You have to be there. Don't worry, it's a very modern country. You don't have to wear a veil. Women drive, go shopping, swim, play golf. At least in the capital."

She wasn't worried about wearing a veil or being able to play golf, which she didn't do, she was worried about being in his country, seeing him with his family and knowing beyond a doubt, once and for all, that she was a fool for falling in love with her boss. Any boss, but especially a boss who was in line to rule a small country one day. Whose family had certain expectations for him.

She'd feel like an outsider. Oh, no doubt they'd be nice to her. She'd heard tales of their legendary hospitality. But she *was* an outsider and it would finally sink in as it never had before.

Maybe that's what she needed. A reality check. Time to stop fantasizing that one day he'd look up from his desk, see her and gasp. *"Claudia, you're beautiful,"* he'd say. *"What's wrong with me? I never knew it before but I'm in love with you."*

She shook her head to clear it from this daydream. It wasn't going to happen. He wasn't in love with her and never would be. As far as she knew he'd never been in love with anyone though not from a lack of opportunity. There were plenty of women who would be only too happy to fall in love with him. Women who were stunningly beautiful and socially prominent. She saw their pictures in the newspaper in the society column. She fielded their phone calls.

If he hadn't fallen for any of them, how did someone like her have a chance with him? She was far from beautiful. She was downright plain. His dates wore glamorous designer clothes, hers were practical and straight off the rack. They had their hair and nails done at salons downtown, she did her own. Their families were the crème de la crème of San Francisco society. Hers was far from that.

She had no intention of changing. Even if she wanted to, how could she? What was the point? Imagine what he'd say if she suddenly turned up like some fashionista in a clingy, form-fitting dress, her hair colored and cut by some high-priced stylist, her face covered with makeup and her feet in stiletto heels.

It should be enough that he respected her, counted on her, depended on her. It had to be enough because that's all it ever would be.

"What's wrong?" he said, leaning over her desk

to look into her eyes. "You were a million miles away. Have you heard a word I've said?"

"Yes, of course," she said, pushing her chair back and standing. She had to get away from that penetrating gaze of his. Away from six feet plus of masculine charm. Away from that voice tinged with just a hint of a foreign accent despite his schooling here and on the continent. This was not the time to argue with him about going to Tazzatine. Not when she was light-headed and dizzy. "I just don't see the need…" she blurted.

"I don't know what you're worried about. The flight is quite comfortable and it's a fascinating country, a blend of old and new. Full of possibilities."

"I know. You told me about the modern city and the desert, the oases and the horses you raise. I'm sure it's beautiful, but…" She held out her hands, palms forward, as if to push him away. As if she could.

"It's a different world from this," he said. "You have to see it to appreciate it. See everything, not just the offshore rigs or the new skyline, not just the desert, or our family villa in the Palmerie. You'll also have the opportunity to meet the people like my family. And the Bayadhi family.

And you'll realize what this deal means to everyone. Yes, you're coming."

All right, maybe she did have to go. Maybe it was the chance of a lifetime to see his world through his eyes. How could she turn him down when he looked at her like that? Those brown eyes so deep and dark a girl could get lost in them. His dark hair falling across his forehead until he brushed it back with an impatient gesture. His jaw clenched tight with determination. Determination. He had enough for ten men. Some called it arrogance, because when Samir Al-Hamri wanted something, he always got it.

"Okay, I'll go," she said.

"I knew I could count on you."

Of course he knew that. When had she ever turned him down for anything whether it was working late, running errands or making excuses for something he didn't want to do? No one said no to Sheikh Samir Al-Hamri. The very idea was preposterous.

"Now I need some coffee," she said, feeling a desperate need to get away and out of his orbit where she was in constant danger of being sucked in and never getting out. "Can I bring you some?"

"Yes, thanks. Cream and two sugars."

She smiled weakly. After two years, he thought

she didn't know how he liked his coffee? Thought she didn't know he liked mustard rather than mayonnaise on his sandwich? Thought she didn't know he preferred Merlot to Cabernet, the circus to the opera, Schumann to Stravinsky?

"Oh, and Claudia?"

She turned and paused at the door.

"Another thing. While we're in Tazzatine…I'm getting engaged."

She grabbed the doorknob with one hand while the room spun around so fast she thought she might pass out. She took a deep breath and forced herself to stay standing and remain calm.

"Congratulations," she blurted. What else could she say? "This is a…a surprise."

"Not really. It's been in the works for a long time. Our families are old friends. This is just a formality."

"Just a formality," she murmured. "How nice." Claudia made it to one of the smooth leather chairs against the wall of her office and sat down. Just for a moment. Just to catch her breath. Just until her legs stopped shaking. It was all she could do to keep her features arranged in an expression of polite interest, no more, no less.

"You're getting engaged," she repeated numbly as if that would help it sink in. Maybe she hadn't heard right. He couldn't possibly be getting engaged, formality or not, without her hearing about it. She saw all his correspondence, took all his phone calls and forwarded his e-mail. "Who is she?"

"She is Zahara Odalya." He reached in his vest pocket and pulled out a picture. Claudia couldn't believe it. He kept a picture of her in his pocket. It made her feel physically sick. Who keeps a photo of his fiancée in his pocket unless he's really in love with her? Her boss in love? It seemed like it. It seemed she had him pegged all wrong.

"Here," he said, handing her a photo of a gorgeous woman with a cloud of dark hair, and a cool expression on her flawless face.

"Oh, she's beautiful," Claudia blurted. How she got that sentence out of her mouth with a lump in her throat the size of Plymouth Rock she had no idea.

"Looks that way."

"You don't know?"

"I haven't seen her for a long time. When I knew her years ago she was a little brat who played with my sister. She went off to school in London while I was in Paris and I never saw her again."

"I'm surprised she isn't married already," Claudia murmured. Anyone who looked like that and was part of Middle Eastern high society should be. What was wrong with her?

He took the photo out of Claudia's hand and studied it with a frown on his face. "So am I. I guess she's been saving herself for me. Why not?" He shrugged. "Everyone agrees it's a good match. Family connections mean everything in our part of the world. You'll see."

No, she wouldn't see. She would not go halfway around the world to see her boss get engaged to someone he didn't love. Or who didn't love him. Or even worse to someone he loved. Or to anyone at all. She might be a loyal employee, but she was no masochist.

"You know, Sam…" It wasn't easy to call him Sam, considering who he was, but he insisted. "I really can't go with you."

He stood there, one eyebrow raised, waiting for her to tell him why she couldn't, so he could tell her why she could. Why she must. Her mind was racing. She had to make it good. He was determined, but so was she.

"I…have a prior commitment."

"What kind of commitment? Your commitment is to me and it's a requirement of your job."

"I know. It always has been, but I'm to be a bridesmaid in my friend Susan's wedding which happens to be right at the same time as this trip you're making." She had a friend named Susan, but she wasn't getting married anytime soon. But how would Sam ever know that? He might not believe her. The look on his face told her he didn't, but he couldn't prove otherwise.

"What a coincidence. Your friend getting married just as the merger takes place. Poor planning on our part I guess. I wonder you didn't mention it before," he said dryly.

"I'm sorry. I guess it slipped my mind. I should have remembered. Because it's June," Claudia said. "Everyone gets married in June."

"Even you?"

Claudia bit her lip. He would have to remind her of her brief marriage, which he only knew about because of the box she'd checked on the application when he hired her. It's not like she ever talked about it or even thought about it very much. "I got married in October and divorced in December. It really doesn't count."

"Is that what this is all about?" he asked, walking to her desk and back again. He always paced when he hit an obstacle in his path as if he could smash it with his feet as he walked. "You had a bad marriage so you're worried about me making the same mistake."

He was so far off the mark she almost laughed.

"I'm sure it won't be the same," she said. Her husband cheated on her even before they got married, then he walked out. There was no way she was going to tell Sam that whole humiliating story. "I'm sure you'll be very happy."

"How can you be so sure?" he asked.

She glanced at the door. Why hadn't she walked out to get coffee before she got embroiled in this no-win argument?

"Because you have no illusions. You're going into this, uh, engagement with your eyes wide-open. You know why you're doing it and so does she."

"And you didn't?"

"I thought I was in love."

"What made you think that?"

She stood and went to the door, determined to get out of the office. "Why does anyone think they're in love?" she asked impatiently. "Their heart beats faster, they daydream, they can't sleep, they can't eat, they can't concentrate. They think they can't survive without the other person."

"Sounds delightful," he said with a sardonic smile. "Glad it's never happened to me."

"You're lucky. You'll never have to suffer."

"The way you did."

She opened her mouth to deny it then stopped. "This is not about me, it's about you. You're the one getting engaged. I'm happy for you. You'll have a lovely party surrounded by your families."

"And you. You'll be there."

"No, I won't. I told you."

"I can't believe you'd even consider this prior commitment. I thought I meant more to you than that. I've always been fair with you, haven't I?" he asked. He leaned back against her desk across the room and leveled the full force of his gaze on her.

She sighed. "Yes."

"I've never asked anything out of bounds. Well, maybe the time you got me out of the bachelor auction by feigning a sudden illness. Everyone felt terrible about it."

"They felt terrible because you missed the auction, not because I was sick."

"That's not true. You got a dozen get-well cards. Now tell me the truth. You owe me that much. There's no wedding. You don't want to come to my country. You don't want to be there when we sign the papers. You aren't interested in my personal life. I understand that and that's okay. But this is primarily a business trip and I want you there. I need you there. Why can't you understand that?"

She did understand. She understood only too well that watching him celebrate his engagement to that beautiful creature in the picture would be like being stabbed in the chest. Might as well throw her in the Gulf with a slab of cement tied to her feet.

"Okay, here's the real reason. I'm afraid to fly. I didn't want to tell you. I thought you would lose respect for me. I know you. You'd make me take fear of flying lessons, or get drugged or see a therapist. But there you have it. I've got acrophobia."

"What is it? Fear of hijacking or turbulence?"

"Yes, all of those."

"Have you seen a doctor?"

"There's no cure for what I've got." The only cure for the common condition of unrequited love was quitting her job, and walking away from the world's sexiest, richest and most gorgeous sheikh. All she had to do was quit. Quit now. Or wait until he was gone, then leave a note on his desk saying…

Sorry, Sam, but I can't work for you anymore. You don't need me anymore. You have Zahara now. All along you knew someday you'd marry her, but you never said a word. When you get engaged, everything will be different. You won't want to work late or phone me at home when you want to talk about business. Nothing will be the same. And I have to get out while I can.

No, she would never do that. Never reveal her true feelings. The best thing to do was lie.

"Maybe it's an ear condition. I'll make you an appointment with a specialist."

"That's not necessary. I'm not going. Someone has to man the office here. That's me." The more determined he was, the more she fought back. For once in her life she would not let him override her. What could he do, tie her up and carry her onto the plane over his shoulder while she pounded on his back and screamed for help? Even he wasn't that determined to get his way. Of course he could fire her for insubordination. Which, if he brought a bride to live here with him, might be doing her a favor by saving her the trouble of resigning.

Images of his fiancée dropping in to say hello and disappearing into his office with him for hours on end made her cringe. Zahara or anyone he married for that matter would call every hour, she'd shove Claudia aside to take over his social schedule, then his business. She'd hire someone else because she'd guess that Claudia was in love with her husband. Women have a second sense that way. Oh, how life can change so drastically in a minute. For the worse.

"We'll hire a temp to answer the phone in here. The rest of the staff will be here," Sam assured her. "They'll cope. We're a small family business."

"A small family business? With offices all over the world and millions in revenues?"

"All right, we're a small office of a large business."

"Now I'm going for coffee," she said.

He flicked his hand in her direction as if she was one of his Arabian horses who wouldn't behave. "Go ahead, but consider our discussion over. You're coming with me and that's settled."

When Claudia came back fifteen minutes later she was armed with a sense of calm resolve and his coffee—cream and two sugars—but he was gone. The note on her desk said he had an appointment. She checked his schedule but couldn't find anything written there for this morning.

She sat at her desk, her chin propped in her hand and stared at the portrait on the wall of his grandfather in his regal headdress next to his favorite horse. Not his wife, his horse. If that didn't give her an idea of family life in Tazzatine, it should. Of course things had changed. But if Sam was getting engaged to someone he didn't love, didn't even know, because it was part of a grand plan for his life, then the old ways were still very much alive.

She'd like to see the country. She'd like to gallop on an Arabian stallion over the dunes. She'd always wanted to sleep in a tent, sip mint tea in the market place, shop for copper pots and take part in the ceremonies that were so much a part of Sam's culture. As long as the ceremonies didn't include his engagement. Sure, he was westernized by his education and his lifestyle, but it was his unique background that made him so much more irresistible than any ordinary man she'd ever met.

If it were just a business trip, she'd be packing her bags by now. She'd be on the phone to the airline. But, it wasn't and surely no woman should have to watch the man she loves get betrothed to someone else.

It was her fault for falling in love with someone so unattainable. What was she thinking? She'd already been ditched and dumped by a rotten jerk. Her ego couldn't take much more, which was why Sam must never ever know how she felt about him.

So far it hadn't been hard to keep her little secret. Even when working late in the office. Even when he drove her home afterward. Even when dropping off important papers at his penthouse condo late at night. But being thrown into contact with him at work and after work in a strange country while he was involved in making plans for his wedding? That was something she didn't need. Not if she valued her sanity. She would not go. No matter what he said she had to get out of it somehow. She hadn't even asked when the wedding was. She didn't want to know.

When the phone rang it was a long distance call from his sister, Amina.

"I'm sorry Samir is not in the office," Claudia said in her personal assistant voice.

"Good, because you're the one I want to talk to, Miss Bradford," Amina said. She lowered her voice. "We have a problem. What I tell you must be a secret. Promise me you won't breathe a word of this to Sam."

Claudia clutched the phone tightly. How could she say no? What was one more secret along with the one she was already keeping?

CHAPTER TWO

"It's about Zahara. You know who I mean?" Amina asked. She sounded worried. Claudia had never had a real conversation with her before. Maybe she always sounded that way.

"His…uh…fiancée?"

"Yes, her. I don't know what to do. The last thing I want is to alarm my brother. He mustn't hear about this. So if someone else calls from here, tell them he's not there. You see she was supposed to try on the engagement party dress I had made for her last week. She postponed, then postponed again. Finally we settled on today, but she didn't show up. She doesn't answer her phone. My other clients who were all asking about her. 'What's happening with Zahara?' they said. 'Haven't seen her for days. Has she got a secret life or something?' I laughed and said something about her being busy."

"That's probably what it is. She's just busy."

"What woman in her right mind is too busy to try on a fabulous new dress for her own engagement party after I designed it and ordered it from Paris and she spent a fortune on alterations?"

"There's so much to do before a big event like this," Claudia suggested. As if she was accustomed to having dresses made for major social events. As if Amina didn't know. Claudia remembered her one and only fitting for her wedding dress and the shower her friend Susan gave her and the rehearsal dinner at the restaurant where Malcolm got drunk. That's when she should have known. That's when she should have pulled the plug on the wedding. She wanted to think she'd changed. That she had more wisdom today than then. Enough wisdom to say no to her boss.

"You don't know her," Amina said. "She has nothing to do. Her servants do it all for her. All she had to do was show up and try on the dress. What's wrong with her? You would think getting engaged to the most eligible man in the country would make her happy, wouldn't you?"

"She's not happy?"

There was a long silence on the other end of the phone. Either Amina was shaking her head or she just didn't know what to say.

Claudia didn't know what to say, either. Should she admit that tying the knot with Sam ought to make anyone delirious with happiness or spout some cliché about how some girls got nervous before a big event?

"What can I do?" Claudia asked at last. Why had Amina called her in the first place? She was thousands of miles away. She was not a friend, not a relative, just an employee.

"Screen his calls. Don't let anyone call and upset the apple cart, if you know what I mean. That includes Zahara. I don't know what she might say. This engagement has been in the works forever. It's fate. Destiny. They're meant to be together. Do you know what it means to our family? Of course you do. You are his most trusted employee. We will be so happy when you arrive. Because Samir has told us how you can fix any problem."

"Well, I'm not sure…" Besides, she thought, what is the problem? If they're really meant for each other, there's no need to worry just because the woman missed her dress fitting.

"He couldn't run his office without you. I don't know what we would do if you weren't coming. If something went wrong and you weren't here…."

Was she talking about the merger or the engagement? Now Claudia was getting confused. It was time for Amina to take a deep breath and calm down.

"Look, Amina, don't worry. Nothing's going to go wrong. All the details have been worked out in advance. The contract is ready to be signed and…"

"Our family has been trying to make this happen for years. We've come close before. Then something always goes wrong. It's as if we're cursed."

"Don't say that. This time it will work." Surely she was talking about the merger.

"Because of you. We never had you on our side before. The fortune teller told me we had to bring in someone new to the negotiations. Someone outside the family. Someone who has never been to our country. Or the deal is doomed. I think she must mean you."

"That's not possible, Amina. She couldn't mean me. She doesn't know me. And I might not…I mean I don't think I can be there."

"You must come."

Determination was obviously a family trait. She'd hate to see a dispute between Sam and his sister.

"Father is very Old-World but he's coming

around to see that women have an important place in the business world. At first he was against me starting my own business. But now I think he's proud of my success. I haven't told him yet what the old crone said to me. But she's never been wrong before."

"She can't have meant me. I'm just an employee with no power or clout," Claudia insisted.

"I don't know but she says she has a message for you when you come here. She's really very good about predictions. You'll see."

Claudia wanted to tell her to spare her the fortune teller's predictions. That she wouldn't be there. That everything would be fine—the merger, the engagement. Everything. And her presence or lack of presence wouldn't make a bit of difference. Except to her. Except to her sanity. But she didn't. She couldn't. Not when Amina was so upset.

There was a knock on her office door and Sam walked in. She said goodbye and hung up quickly.

"Who was that?" Sam asked when she hung up.

"My friend Sharon." What was one more lie at this point?

"I hope she wasn't too disappointed you won't be at her wedding."

Claudia sighed.

He smiled because he knew he'd won. He always won. "You won't be sorry about this, Claudia. Now, I have a favor to ask."

Claudia looked up. A favor? Wasn't traveling to his country to be on hand for a merger signing and an engagement favor enough? The confident smile on his face told her whatever it was, he was sure she wouldn't say no. Not after she'd just as good as said yes to his plan.

"I went out looking for a ring for my fiancée. Obviously I can't show up without one, but I have no idea what to buy. You have good taste. Take the afternoon off. Go to Tiffany's. I have an account there. Get me a ring. Something with diamonds. Something large but not ostentatious. You know what women like."

Claudia froze. Just when she thought things couldn't get worse, they did.

Two weeks later, despite every fiber in her body crying out to her that it was a mistake, she was on the plane, sitting in first-class next to Sam who had a stunning five-carat ring from Tiffany's in his pocket and a sheaf of papers spread out on the tray table in front of him.

She had papers to look at, too, but he'd insisted

she take the window seat and she couldn't resist looking down at the world below, islands in a blue sea, mountains and forests, imagining the lives of the people down there. Picturing them getting married, having children, growing up, leaving home.

Most of all she wondered how she was going to get through the coming days without losing her composure, without bursting into uncontrollable crying or shouting out how wrong this whole engagement was. But what did she know? She was a divorced woman, an outsider without the background to judge such things. Obviously arranged marriages often worked out better than so-called love matches.

On what grounds could she object?

This man doesn't love this woman.

This man doesn't know this woman.

This man doesn't believe in love.

This is a business arrangement, not a marriage.

She could just hear the derisive laughter. The pitying looks the family would give her. How naïve she was, thinking marriage should be about love. Maybe they were right.

One thing she didn't have to worry about was the fiancée and her dress. Amina called again with the message that the problem was solved. No details. But obviously Zahara had appeared, tried on her dress and everyone was relieved, including Claudia.

Yes, what a relief to know Sam would be happily engaged within the week. If not happily then dutifully. As far as she knew happiness had nothing to do with this union. It was a duty. Knowing that didn't help Claudia's state of mind. She had no idea how she was going to handle seeing him actually slip the diamond ring on her finger in the traditional ceremony he'd mentioned. Just the thought of it gave her a pain between her ribs.

If he was concerned about pledging to marry someone he scarcely knew, he didn't let on. The only thing he seemed to be worried about was the agreement between the families. Which was why he was engrossed in the documents in front of him. Making sure nothing could go wrong.

At lunchtime the flight attendant brought them each a Salade Nicoise which Sam had specially ordered. Claudia watched the attendant toss tuna, potatoes and green beans in a light vinaigrette sauce then serve it individually in a bed of butter lettuce. It was absolutely delicious and she enjoyed every bite along with a crusty roll and a glass of chilled white wine.

"You seem to be over your acrophobia," Sam said with a sideways glance at her.

She'd completely forgotten about it. How like him to remember.

"Yes, thank you. It must be first-class." She looked around at the well-dressed passengers, sipping wine or coffee, their laptop computers in front of them. "No one would dare be sick up here."

"First time?"

"First time in a plane in any class."

His mouth curved in a half smile.

"The first time I flew was a trip I made with my mother and my sister when we were very young to our mother's home in France," he said pensively.

"You've never mentioned your mother," she said.

"Perhaps because she moved back to Provence when my sister and I went off to boarding school."

"Then your parents are divorced?"

"Yes. I know what you're thinking. That arranged marriages don't always work out. But theirs was a love match. They met at university in France. But my mother didn't know what she was getting in to. She was swept off her feet by my father. He was very dashing and very persuasive.

"She was always homesick and lonely in Tazzatine. My father didn't know how to deal with her problem. He turned our house in the palmerie into a tropical villa and hired a French chef, but it just made her more homesick than ever. He never understood why she couldn't adjust. I think the only reason she stuck it out as long as she did was because of us children. When we left home for school, she did, too."

"I'm sorry," Claudia said, thinking of him growing up without a mother. Impulsively she put her hand on his arm.

"Don't be. She's much happier now than she's ever been."

"Are you?" she asked. Even though they never discussed personal matters and it was none of her business, she asked anyway.

"Of course," he said. "You should know that. And so is Amina. She spent last summer with my mother on holiday in the south of France. And I see her when I can."

He shifted in his seat and she took her hand away. Maybe he didn't want her sympathy. Maybe he was sorry he'd confided in her at all. "We have strong extended families in our country. When one person leaves, another fills in. In this case it was my aunt who moved in with us," he continued.

"I see."

"On that trip we took to France I realized then how much my mother had given up to marry my father. And how difficult her life was away from friends and family, a stranger in a strange land. And you wonder why I don't put much store in the idea of love?" he asked. "Look at all the problems it causes."

Claudia didn't want to get into an argument about love. What did she know about it? All love had done for her was to cause her pain, and the worst was likely still to come.

Fortunately he changed the subject. "How does it happen you've never flown before?"

"There didn't seem to be any reason to fly and I was always afraid," she said a little defensively. But now sitting next to Sam who oozed confidence and assurance, she wasn't afraid of flying or anything. Whatever happened, he'd take care of it. The die was cast. She was on her way. There was nothing more she could do about it. No more protests. No more telling him it was really ridiculous for her to make this trip. She had to grin and bear whatever came.

Sure, she was the details girl, but with communications between countries being lightning fast, she could have dealt with any problem from San

Francisco. No matter what she said, he had an answer for it. The time for arguing was over. They were on their way.

When the attendant removed the plates, she leaned back in her chair and told herself to enjoy the flight. Enjoy having Sam to herself while she could, discussing his childhood or his country or his family, just the two of them. It wouldn't last.

Not only did she enjoy talking to him for the hours in the air about geography, weather, the shipping business and his plans for the future of the company, but she also enjoyed the hot fudge sundae they served for dessert.

"I've never seen you eat so much," Sam said, a smile on his face. "I don't think I've ever known a woman who wasn't on a diet."

"Now you do," she said. But of course he didn't know her at all. Not really.

"Aren't you afraid you won't fit into your dress?"

"What dress?"

"The one you're wearing to the engagement party."

"I...I don't think I brought anything suitable. I never thought of it but, that's okay, I'd be out of place with all your friends and family anyway."

"My sister will find you something. She has a

dress shop and she loves anything to do with fashion."

"Really?"

"You'll like her."

"I'm sure I will."

Sam was puzzled. From the moment they'd stepped aboard the plane Claudia seemed different. Even though she thought she had acrophobia, she obviously didn't. She seemed to relax once they took their seats. Not the way someone would if they were afraid of flying. Maybe she was relieved to have the bulk of the work done. He'd kept her busy these past weeks, that he knew.

She always worked hard, so did he, but this time they really threw themselves into it, staying late at the office, ordering sandwiches and coffee so they wouldn't have to leave until every "t" was crossed and every "i" dotted. Then just when he thought everything was in order, there was a last minute change from his father's lawyers. He didn't know what he'd do without Claudia.

He watched her adjust her seat and look out the window. He'd made this trip so many times he no longer got a thrill out of the service, the food or the views from thirty thousand feet in the air. He'd forgotten what it was like to experience it for the first time. Until she mentioned it, he'd forgotten about that first flight he'd made with his mother and it made him nostalgic for a few moments.

He leaned toward Claudia to look out the window. He brushed her arm and inhaled the faint scent of roses. Roses at thirty thousand feet? Perfume on Claudia, his no-nonsense assistant? It wasn't possible.

When he got his bearings, he explained to her where they were, pointed out Hudson Bay below, at the ice and snow-covered land formed tens of thousands of years ago. Told her what an incredible contrast it would be when they landed in a country one hundred and fifty Fahrenheit degrees hotter than the one they were above, and almost completely covered with sand.

"What about the oases?" she asked.

"Those are mere depressions in the sand. A spring, a village with a few houses and some palm trees. I hope you won't be disappointed."

"Not at all. I've seen the pictures. They look amazing."

He nodded. It would be interesting to see what she really thought of the palm-fringed, spring-fed Moroccan-style villa where the family went on vacation. Maybe it would strike Claudia as isolated as it had his mother, considering his assistant had spent her whole life in an American city. Maybe its charms would be lost on her, too. He wondered if there'd be time to take her to the villa or if she'd really want to go. Maybe they'd be too busy.

She took out her new camera and snapped some pictures of the view, then she asked more questions. Who owned the land beneath them? Did anyone live there? He didn't know all the answers. He opened his laptop and looked for maps and information to share with her. Then he answered some important e-mail. She opened her newspaper and started a crossword puzzle. Unable to concentrate, he looked over her shoulder.

"Four letter word for mid-east ruler," he read aloud. "Emir."

She wrote the letters in pencil. "Is that you?" she asked.

He shook his head. "An emir is a prince. I'm just a sheikh. In line to be head of our tribe, which is about half the country. But not until my father dies. In the meantime I'm just another hardworking executive who depends on his assistant to do all the hard work."

Her cheeks flushed and turned a becoming

pink. She was always so composed, he liked catching her off guard, surprising her when he could with a compliment she didn't expect. She was the most modest woman he'd ever met. He wondered if she possessed even a twinge of vanity. Except for the scent of roses. He was tempted to ask about that, but he didn't want to embarrass her any further.

"I'm not the only one who compliments you, am I?" he asked. He really had no idea of what her life outside the office was like. Maybe it was just like his. Work, eat, sleep and more work.

"My knitting club thinks I do good work," she said primly.

"Really. What do you knit?"

"Socks. Scarves. Sweaters."

"So that's what you do in your spare time, knit?"

"I don't have much spare time."

"That's my fault. I work you too hard."

"You work just as hard or harder. Maybe after…"

"Maybe after I get married, all that will change. Is that what you were going to say?"

"When are you getting married?" she asked.

"I don't know. Whenever it's convenient, I suppose."

"It's possible your wife will have plans for you.

Like where you'll live. What you'll do in the evenings besides work."

He frowned. He simply hadn't thought beyond the merger and the engagement announcement. He had no wish to change his residence, or anything about his life. He didn't want someone bringing in new furniture, making plans for him, or taking up his spare time such as it was. What would Zahara expect? A long engagement, he hoped, postponing any difficult decisions for some time to come. Would she even want to live in San Francisco? Maybe she'd stay where she was, wherever that was. Why not?

He assumed everything in his life would stay the same except his family and Zahara's family would be satisfied. As for the business merger, the company would now be twice as large. Twice as many opportunities. Twice as much clout in the worldwide shipping business.

"As far as work goes, the only changes will be for the better, I'm sure," he said. "You may need an assistant."

She didn't say anything. She probably hadn't considered their workload might be heavier. But she knew him well enough to know that when he wanted something he made it happen. If he didn't want his life to change, it wouldn't. If they needed help, he'd hire more people. Still she looked dubious, or maybe it was just that she couldn't figure out number ten down.

"Four letters, a super model," she murmured.

He said a name that she vaguely recognized.

She slanted a glance in his direction. "You know about models?"

"Tall, skinny girls with bony hips and cheek-bones? I know I prefer women with curves. Women who smile once in a while."

Claudia herself smiled at his description.

He had no idea if she had curves or not. Not under the shapeless suits she wore to the office and here on the plane. Too bad she hadn't thought to bring a dress for the party. Maybe he should have told her to. But that wasn't his job to tell his assistant what to wear. Still, he wondered what she'd look like in a party dress. He couldn't imagine.

He thought about Zahara. What had happened to her since the last time he saw her? Did she smile? Did she have curves? How did she really feel about this engagement? Did she accept it as he did as a done deal? Would she be at the airport to meet him?

She was not at the airport. His father sent a driver, a man who'd been with him for years. Sam looked around and wondered what Claudia thought of seeing a sea of men in white robes all talking at full volume. It must be overwhelming. He thought of his mother and what she must have felt. Ali, the driver bowed slightly and said, "Welcome home," before he picked up their bags from the luggage carousel.

Home? Was this hot, muggy city home? Or was it San Francisco often covered in a blanket of cool, damp fog? Or didn't he have a home anymore? With his suit jacket over his shoulder and his shirtsleeves rolled up, he and Claudia followed Ali through customs and out to the waiting limousine.

Claudia fanned her face with her customs form. She had a sheen of perspiration on her face.

"The limo's air-conditioned," he said. She must be feeling the heavy humidity, so different from the city they'd left behind.

In minutes they were parked in front of the office. He got out of the car, looked up and shaded his eyes from the relentless sun. There were more high-rise buildings since his last visit. And more going up every day. The whirring of cranes, the clanging of steel beams and the chattering of air hammers filled the air. It all meant progress.

He slanted a glance in Claudia's direction. How

did it look to a stranger? Was she in culture shock already from the heat and the noise? If so, she didn't show it. She stepped briskly into the cool lobby of the Al-Hamri Building and followed him to the elevator as if she'd been doing it every day of her life.

He left Claudia in the lobby with his father's assistant and went straight to the old man's office where he embraced him.

"Father, how are you?" Just a glance at the old man had Sam worried. He looked older, tired and when Sam wrapped his arms around him he seemed thin and frail. How had this happened in the six months since he'd seen him in Hamburg at the launching of their new container ship? Shouldn't someone have told him if his father wasn't well?

"Fine, now that you're here." Abdul Al-Hamri smiled at Sam and sat down in his large leather chair, the same chair where his grandfather had once sat. Not here. Not in this modern high-rise. What would his grandfather have thought if he could see what Sam saw when he looked out the window at the huge oil rigs just offshore and the miles of new buildings?

"How was the plane trip?"

"We were able to get some work done."

"We?"

"I brought my assistant with me. Claudia. She's indispensable in negotiations."

The old man's face was creased in a frown. "Who?"

Sam surveyed his father with a worried look. He'd mentioned Claudia before. He knew he had. He'd told him she was coming with him. Was his father's memory going?

"I've told you about her. She's been working with me for two years. She's my right-hand man, so to speak. She understands our situation better than anyone who's not family. I rely on her and trust her implicitly."

His father shook his head.

"Surely you don't still believe a woman's place is in the home," Sam said. "Not in today's world. Look at Amina, running her own shop."

"I know. I know. Things are changing. Truthfully I would prefer that Amina get married and stay home to raise a family. But she has a mind of her own, like you. Like her mother."

"And like you, Father. She's inherited much of your drive and ambition." Surely it would please his father to hear that.

"God help her," his father muttered. "The country's changing so fast it makes me wonder.

Is it all for the best? There's something to be said for the old ways, for tradition. For marriage and family," he added pointedly. "That's why you're here, isn't it? Besides the business agreement."

"Of course." But Sam felt his muscles tense. Back in California marriage was far off. This was just an engagement, but now they were talking about marriage and family and not in the abstract. His father meant *his* marriage and *his* family.

Sam wasn't ready to think about that. Not yet. Now that he was there in Tazzatine the idea of marrying a stranger was far from appealing.

"How is Zahara?" Sam asked politely.

"I don't know. I haven't seen her. Either has her father."

Sam frowned. They hadn't seen her? What did that mean? "Is there a problem?" he asked.

His father shot him a querulous glance. "Of course not. I have been assured that everything is in order."

After just a short conversation Sam realized he and his father were not entirely in agreement on the direction the country was taking, the role of women and the responsibility of their family to their country. But these were issues they could continue to discuss and hopefully come to some accommodation. In their phone conversations they never got into any controversial subjects at all. But face-to-face, it was hard to avoid such topics. It was best to talk business.

"In any case, the contract is almost ready to sign," his father said. "As soon as business is finished your assistant will get a chance to enjoy herself by shopping or playing golf. Amina will take care of her when you and I are busy. There are just a few, last-minute changes they've asked for. I said I would have to run them by you. Then it's just a matter of the signing ceremony. And the engagement party of course. You don't know how happy this makes me. And the Odalyas of course. Ben Abdul Odalya is my oldest friend in the world. We always hoped… Although…"

Sam waited, but his father only stared straight ahead lost in thought.

"Are you sure everyone is happy about the engagement?" Sam said. He was beginning to wonder why his father was so vague about it.

"Sit down," his father said. "There is something I need to ask you."

Claudia felt like Alice who'd just dropped down the rabbit hole and landed in Wonderland. Outside the temperature must be close to ninety degrees with matching humidity and inside this building the air-conditioning was turned up so high she was shivering.

She expected a boom town, she didn't expect the loud noise of jackhammers and so much dust swirling outside on the street, so many white buildings reflecting the dazzling bright sunshine, so many men and women dressed in the latest European fashions alongside the women in veils and men in the traditional keffiyeh.

After a tour of the offices, a tall, slim young woman in a smart black suit appeared and introduced herself as Amina. She shook Claudia's hand and smiled warmly.

"You must be exhausted after your flight. Where's my brother? Ah, I know, in with Father. Come with me. You're staying in my apartment. You'll want to unpack and rest up before the party."

Party? Surely she wasn't expected to go to a party so soon. "I shouldn't leave without telling Sam." And telling him she was there to work and only to work. Why else had she come all this way?

"We aren't going far. The family apartments are on the top floor. It's more convenient that way, especially for the workaholics in my family." She smiled to soften the implied criticism. "I'll leave word where he can find us. Those men, once they start talking about ships and freight, they lose track of time. I must remind them of the dinner party tonight. The Bayadhis will be there of course as well as Zahara's family. Because we're celebrating the engagement as well as the merger. A lot of strange faces all at once, I know, but I hope you'll have a good time."

A good time at a family affair where the man she loved got engaged to someone else? Not likely. Claudia had no wish to intrude on this happy occasion. Besides she needed some time to pull herself together. She had to get out of it. "Please don't worry about including me. I'll be fine on my own."

"But of course you will dine with us." Amina signaled to a young man upon which he picked up Claudia's bag and walked out the door.

Claudia opened her mouth to make an excuse, but she knew better than to cross a strong-willed member of the Al-Hamri family, whether it was Amina or her brother.

"Very convenient indeed," Claudia remarked when Amina whisked them up in the private elevator to her apartment. It was more than convenient. It was beautiful.

The furniture was antique, comfortable but

elegant, very much what a well-heeled single woman might have in New York or even Paris. Amina left her shoes at the door and Claudia did the same. Her hostess told Claudia the carpets and the colorful wall hangings were hand-woven by local artisans. When Claudia admired them, Amina said she'd take her shopping in the souks where she knew the merchants by first name.

Amina threw open the French doors to the balcony to let the sea breeze in. Claudia stepped outside and took a deep breath. What a relief to get away from the chill of the omnipresent air-conditioning. The waters of the Gulf glittered in the late afternoon sunlight.

"You must have work to do," Claudia said to Amina. "Please don't let me distract you. I don't need to be entertained. I can do very well on my own."

"I have an assistant in the shop this afternoon," Amina said. "I have been looking forward to this meeting with you. Now that you are here I can breathe easier. So can we all."

"I don't understand. I'm only here in case there are any last-minute problems with the agreement." She hoped the rantings of a superstitious fortune teller had been forgotten.

Amina nodded slowly. A woman in a simple

long dress came out to the balcony with two glasses of tamarind juice and small bowls of nuts and olives she placed on a wrought-iron table.

"Thank you, Fatima," Amina said, then waited until the maid had left the balcony and gone back inside before she spoke.

"Problems?" she said with a rueful smile. "Ah, yes, if you only knew."

CHAPTER THREE

THE GUEST ROOM was done in pale green and soft peach and had its own balcony overlooking the sea below. It was feminine but not a fussy room. A king-size canopy bed was outfitted with one hundred percent Egyptian cotton sheets and butter-soft pale peach blankets. But Amina's real pride and joy was the guest bathroom.

"My aunts scoff and say it's too old-fashioned for their taste. But that is why I like it. I ordered everything from England, the porcelain-glazed sink, the cast-iron claw-foot tub and the white tiles on the wall. I hope you like it."

"Like it? I love it. It's charming," Claudia said. It was more than charming. It was fully outfitted with luxury towels, a fluffy bathrobe, an antique wall phone and a TV hidden behind a mirror. Now she knew she was in Wonderland. The only thing lacking was the mad Queen of Hearts. Would she meet her tonight?

Amina smiled. "I'm glad you like it. I hope you like it so much you will stay a long time."

"Oh, no, I don't think I can. Back in California the work is piling up in our absence. We must get back soon."

Amina nodded, but Claudia wondered if she'd really heard her. Sam's sister seemed preoccupied. She hadn't explained what she meant by that "problems" remark. Instead she opened the walk-in closet in the guest room where a silky negligee hung on a hanger next to a matching dressing gown.

"What will you wear to the party tonight?" Amina asked.

"I…I'm afraid I have nothing appropriate," Claudia said, opening her suitcase, which the servant had deposited on the wicker luggage rack and surveying the contents with apprehension. What had she been thinking, packing only work clothes? She had been under the impression this was a work trip, not a vacation, that's what she had been thinking.

"So you see, all the more reason I shouldn't attend. I wouldn't know anyone and the truth is, I'm not much of a party person." That was an understatement. Even if she'd been told she would have to attend the party, what would she have brought? The fanciest outfit she owned was a dark suit and a silk blouse, not much different from the dark suit, cotton blouse and low-heeled shoes she'd worn for traveling. Or that she wore every day to work.

"Never mind. You'll wear something of mine." Amina looked her up and down. "I dare say we're about the same size, don't you think? In a minute I'll bring in some things for you to try on. You do know I run a dress shop, don't you? It's my job to dress women. I'm not bragging but I like to think I do a good job of it. For me it's not just my job, it's my passion."

Once again Claudia saw the similarity between Amina and her brother. They each had a passion for what they did and she envied that. Amina sat in an armchair covered with luxuriously embossed fabric and tucked her legs under her. "What is yours?"

"My…my passion?" Claudia sat on the edge of the bed. "I knit and I belong to a book club, but mostly I have no time for a passion. I spend long hours working."

Amina frowned. "That is my brother's fault. I must speak to him about that."

"No, please don't. I love my job." As if speaking to Sam would change her brother's work habits.

"Very well," she said. "If you say so. Now I will bring you the dresses for the party."

"I appreciate the offer, but I probably wouldn't fit into your dresses and I wouldn't fit in at your party, either. I don't know anyone and…"

"You're shy, yes?" Amina smiled sympathetically. "That's what Samir told us."

Claudia's eyes widened. "He told you about me?"

"Of course. How hard you work, how devoted you are to him and the company. How he cannot get along without you. And there's the fortune teller who seems to know you as well." Amina tilted her head to one side. "Yes, you are exactly the way I pictured you."

For some reason this wasn't exactly what Claudia wanted to hear. The person she described sounded incredibly boring. Which was exactly what Sam must think of her. She was just a part of the business, one he couldn't do without to be sure, like the fax machine, or the copier. Suddenly she felt very very tired. She looked longingly at the four-poster bed and then at her watch. No wonder. It was midnight in California.

"Lie down," Amina commanded. "Take a nap.

Get some rest while you can. Before the fun starts," she added with a smile.

Fun? Hardly, but she was here, and she would have to do whatever it took to keep her emotions under control. When fatigue finally overtook her she stretched out on the smooth, silky bedspread. Just for a moment.

When she awoke the sun was setting and turning the sea to gold. She felt disoriented, sure it must be morning, but where? Not here.

She looked around to find the room full of filmy dresses in an array of colors, lying on the chair, hanging in the closet and folded at the end of the bed and a stack of shoe boxes on the floor.

Ah, yes, now she recalled. A sinking feeling hit her. Clothes. A party. An agreement. And an engagement.

"There you are." It was Amina, smiling at her from the doorway, wearing a long, loose dress they called the djellaba, her hair pulled back from her face. "Feeling better? You look it. Sam called. He asked how you were doing. I told him you were napping."

Claudia sat up straight and ran her hand through her hair. Sam needed her and she was sleeping. "You should have woken me. Maybe he needed to talk to me."

"Whatever it was can wait," Amina said. "You look rested. Rested enough to receive Durrah, the fortune teller?"

"You mean she's here?" Claudia was definitely not feeling like herself, but what harm could it do to listen to a fortune teller? She knew what she'd say. What they all said. You will meet a tall, dark stranger. You will travel across the sea. And so on. Even though Amina swore this one was special, that she'd already predicted things about her, Claudia was skeptical to say the least.

"First I'd better speak to Sam," she said.

Amina nodded and handed her her cell phone.

"Is everything okay?" she asked when he answered her call.

"More or less," he said. "I'm glad you were able to get some rest. It's going to be a big night."

"So it seems." A big night for him and his family, no doubt, but a horrible long night for her. She must not spoil this occasion by complaining or telling him she didn't want to attend.

"Is Amina taking good care of you?" he asked.

"She couldn't be nicer. She's even provided a fortune teller for entertainment."

Amina grinned and nodded toward the door as if the woman was waiting there.

"Don't tell me you believe in that nonsense," he said sternly.

"It will be interesting to hear what she has to say," Claudia said tactfully with an eye on Amina. She didn't want to discount his sister's fortune teller before she'd even met her.

"I can tell you what she'll say," Sam said. "Because Amina forced me to endure a session with the so-called fortune teller the last time I was here. She'll look at your palm and tell you you have a deep, long line stretching horizontally across your palm, which means you have clear and focused thinking. Which you already know because I've told you a thousand times. What a waste of time."

"Yes, well, thanks for your input. I'll see you soon then."

"I suppose Sam told you his feelings about fortune tellers," Amina said when Claudia had hung up. "My brother is the most cynical of men, as you no doubt know. He doesn't believe in seers, magicians, or anything he can't see and touch. Like love for example. Mark my words, someday he'll fall and when he does I will have the last laugh."

Claudia smiled politely. She had to agree that Sam was cynical, but as for him falling in love, if it hadn't happened yet, it didn't seem likely.

Durrah the fortune teller was small and dark and draped in a long, colorful garment. Her fingers were covered with jeweled rings. Claudia smiled to herself. This woman couldn't have looked more the part of fortune teller than if she'd been cast and costumed for a Hollywood movie.

Durrah waved to Claudia to join her at the small table where she made herself comfortable in one of the wing chairs and set a deck of cards in front of her. Amina leaned back against the dressing table. "To translate," she explained.

The first thing Durrah did was to study Claudia's palms. Sure enough, she did tell Claudia she had a deep, long "head" line, which meant clear and focused thinking. But she moved on to examine her broken "heart" line and told her it meant disappointment in love.

Claudia, feeling a little uncomfortable, shifted in her chair. Disappointment was not quite the word for what Claudia had gone through. Durrah couldn't possibly know about her divorce. It was just a good guess. After all, most people had been disappointed in love at one time or another. But Claudia was a guest and she must not let her cynicism show no matter what she thought. It would be rude.

When the woman turned to her cards, Claudia

was relieved. She had been hitting too close to home when she had zeroed in on Claudia's love line.

"She says there is trouble ahead," Amina said. "Someone is sick."

"Oh, dear. Not someone in your family, I hope," Claudia said.

"No, but it will affect the family."

"What about the merger?" Claudia asked. After all, what could be more important?

"She can't see it. It doesn't mean it won't happen, it just means she's having trouble picturing it." Amina frowned. "Well, no one can be right all the time," she murmured. "But there's more. She wants to tell you there's a man in your future."

"Really?" Claudia asked politely. "Is he tall and dark?"

"Why yes," Amina said. "That's exactly right. She says you will find happiness and wealth beyond your wildest dreams. It will be soon. And it will be nearby."

"Nearby?" Claudia asked, glancing around the room. The woman must be getting desperate.

Amina nodded. "The disappointment you once felt will fade like the broken heart line on your palm. And you will live happily ever after. A long, long life. Now, aren't you happy you came here?"

"As long as we can accomplish what we came to do, then of course I'll be happy," Claudia said. Surely Amina didn't believe that a fortune teller, no matter how gifted she was, was capable of spouting anything but tried and true clichés.

"And now it's time to try on some party dresses," she said, handing Durrah a small purse and showing her to the door.

"Wait." The old woman stopped in the doorway, her jeweled hand held high in the air. Amina translated what she had to say. "A woman can hide her love for forty years but her disgust and anger not for one day." She wagged her finger at Claudia. "Remember this."

Claudia smiled politely but inside she was trembling. Surely the woman didn't know anything. How could she possibly guess Claudia had a love to hide at all? She breathed a sigh of relief when Amina closed the door.

"I'm not sure what that was all about," Amina said, then she threw herself into the process of selecting a dress for Claudia. "Maybe it will be revealed to us in time."

Claudia had never been much of a shopper, but she'd rather try on dresses for hours than hear any more of the fortune teller's ramblings. Who knew what more she'd say about her love life if she had any encouragement?

She'd only known Sam's sister for a matter of hours, but Claudia was once again struck by the Al-Hamri family resemblance and it wasn't just Amina's dark expressive eyes that were like her brother's, or her smooth, ebony hair or her passion for her work. It was her manner, her way of setting an agenda and making decisions for others, like what Claudia should wear to the party.

When she disagreed with Sam, sometimes Claudia took a stand, sometimes it just wasn't worth it. She'd learned working with him to pick her battles. The battle of the party dress was not one she was willing to fight over. She might as well give in this time, wear a dress and go to the party.

Good thing she'd decided to give in, because Amina was busily unzipping dresses, holding them out and insisting Claudia strip down to her underwear. Which she could tell by the look on her face, Amina did not find acceptable. Who wore all cotton briefs besides Claudia? Who didn't wear pretty lacy bikinis or demi bras? Claudia didn't. And she had no intention of changing. But she hadn't counted on the Al-Hamri resolve.

It seemed Amina had a collection of lingerie for

sale at her shop on hand right there in her apartment, which she insisted Claudia try on. Next it was the dresses.

Sam rang the bell on his sister's door, but when she didn't answer, he let himself in with his key. His own apartment was just across the hall.

"Hello," he called, "anyone home?"

He followed the sound of girlish laughter down the hall from the bedrooms.

"Amina? Claudia?" he said.

"Back here, Sam," his sister answered.

In her guest bedroom he found his sister sitting on the floor, her arms around her knees looking at a woman he scarcely recognized as his assistant who was standing in the middle of the room wearing a bright red dress. It couldn't be Claudia.

Claudia in a bright red cocktail dress that came just below her knees showing long and shapely legs he'd never noticed before. Because if he'd seen those legs, he would have noticed. Maybe it was the high-heeled shoes she was wearing. Totally unlike her. Where had those come from?

He leaned against the wall and stuffed his hands into his pockets. He was tired, hungry and jet-lagged, and now this. Too many changes in too short a time left him feeling like he'd been thrown off his favorite stallion and landed on his head.

"Like it?" his sister asked.

"Very nice," he said. What else could he say? *I don't want my assistant looking sexy. I can't handle that right now. So take the dress off of her and get her back into her work uniform—dark suit, white blouse and sensible shoes.*

Nice? He would never admit it out loud, but she was stunning in this red dress that was so unlike anything Claudia would normally wear that he rubbed his eyes in disbelief.

"Where's the fortune teller?" he asked. "I thought that's what you were up to."

"She was here," Amina said. "Just long enough to tell us there's a tall, dark man in Claudia's future as well as wealth and happiness. Isn't that right, Claudia?"

Sam frowned. Claudia in a bright red dress with a tall, dark stranger? This was complete foolishness. Fortunately his assistant was as sensible as she was or her head might be turned. "No one in her right mind would believe that old crone," Sam said. "And Claudia is definitely in her right mind. She's the brightest woman I know." He knew how lucky he was to have her for an assistant. As soon as she got out of that dress, things would be back to normal and she'd be back in the role she always occupied.

"Think what you will, Sam," Amina said. "We'll see who's right. You may have to swallow your cynical comments when the future is revealed."

He held out his hands. "You know me. I'm as open-minded as the next man. If it comes true, I'll admit I was wrong. No one deserves wealth and happiness more than Claudia."

"What about the tall, dark stranger?" Amina asked. "Does she deserve him?"

"If that's what she wants." He looked at Claudia who looked uncomfortable in the extreme. He could not imagine Claudia waiting around for a stranger to lure her away with wealth and happiness. If he did, she might quit and where would Sam be without her? Stuck trying to get by without his right-hand man, that's where.

"I hope you didn't pay much for this ridiculous prediction," Sam said, looking at his sister then at Claudia.

"It's not ridiculous at all," Amina said, her hands on her hips. "Claudia is a lovely woman. She could meet someone special and rich at any time and succumb to his charms. In fact, considering the wealth per capita in our country, I believe she's come to the right place to see her fortune fulfilled. She doesn't belong to you, Sam. She just works for you."

Sam turned to take another look at Claudia. Just worked for him? All right, maybe she did look lovely in the dress. That didn't mean she was any more susceptible to the flattery of a stranger. In fact, she was beginning to look tired around the eyes and her mouth was drooping. This was all his sister's fault.

"Enough of this," he said. "You've had your fun, Amina. Let my assistant get out of this dress."

Amina stood and picked up a hanger. "If you'll excuse us, Sam, we are still looking at dresses. What about this leopard print, for example."

Sam shook his head. A leopard print on Claudia? Things were getting out of hand. Amina held up a strapless dress, then tossed it on the bed and grabbed another. "Champagne peau de soie with scoop neck and bubble skirt, one of my personal favorites."

Amina turned to Claudia. "Which one do you like best?"

Sam stared at her. All she had to do was say— *None of the above. I don't want to wear a sexy party dress. It's not my style.* But she didn't. She said she liked the red one. Had she lost her mind? Clearly he'd been mistaken in leaving her in the care of his strong-willed sister.

Claudia seemed to be unaware of how outrageous she looked. She was staring at herself in the full-length mirror on the closet door with a strange, puzzled expression on her face. Her cheeks were flushed and her hair was in a tangle, so unlike her usual tailored self he was almost speechless.

"Claudia, don't let Amina tell you what to wear," he said. "She gets carried away with her power over her customers."

"Don't talk to me about using my power," Amina said with a saucy grin at her brother. "I think I know a bit more than you about what looks good on women."

"You love doing this, don't you?" he asked his sister. "You used to dress your dolls, now you dress women the same way."

Amina chuckled. His sister never took anything he said seriously. "Nothing wrong with that, is there?" she said. "Making beautiful women more beautiful. It's a gift I have, if I may say so myself."

Maybe it was her gift, but Claudia was not a beautiful woman. She was practical, smart and intuitive. Not unattractive, but no one would call her beautiful. He should never have left Claudia alone with Amina. Look what happened.

He took a step back. As if he got too close to

his assistant in this red dress she was wearing, he might get burned.

"Oh, there's my phone. Be right back." Amina dashed down past Sam and hurried down the hall.

"How did your meeting go?" Claudia asked Sam. "You said you wanted to talk to me."

"Well…" He simply couldn't concentrate with her standing there in that dress. Was he the only one who noticed it didn't suit her at all?

"Have their been any changes?"

"A few." He walked to the French doors that opened to the balcony and looked out to sea. "The biggest change is in my father. He's not himself. I don't know what to do. He's feeling his age, I'm afraid. Which is why the merger is somewhat worrying. The company will be huge and he'll have that much more responsibility."

"That's too bad. Maybe someone from the other family can step in to pick up the slack."

Sam didn't look convinced. "Perhaps. It's true that control for the new company has to be shared if this merger is to work. But it's going to be hard to give up total control and put trust in others."

"Isn't that true of marriage as well?" she asked softly.

He turned to look at her, struck once again by her intuitive powers. "Of course. I hadn't made the connection, but you're right, as usual," he said. "Maybe that's why I never wanted to get married." *And still don't.*

"It will take some time to reorganize, I imagine," she said.

"The company or the marriage?" he asked.

She didn't say anything. He knew the answer was "both" as well as she did.

"Let's get back to business," he said brusquely. This conversation was getting entirely too personal. "You'll make one of your brilliant organizational charts so we can get an idea where we all fit in…to the company of course." She had a genius for sorting things out and making complicated matters understandable. As long as they had nothing to do with his personal life. He would handle that in his own way. Or put it off as long as possible.

"I'd be glad to. I'm looking forward to meeting your father," she said.

"Good," Sam said. Once his father met her, he'd realize what an asset she was. After he saw her in action, he'd be as impressed as Sam himself was with Claudia's knowledge and perception. "You'll meet him tonight."

He took another look at her from her tousled hair to her high-heeled shoes, hoping he'd made a mistake and the dress hadn't changed her after all. She sounded the same. She thought the same. But she didn't look the same. He'd never seen such a transformation within the space of a few hours. It was Amina's doing. Her fault. On her own Claudia would never have chosen to wear a dress like this.

"So is this really what you're wearing tonight?"

"Amina says the party is a formal occasion, so…"

"She knows fashion and I don't. I just think…"

"It's too much, isn't it? It's too bright, too…too…everything. It isn't really me." Her eyes, which had been so bright, now avoided his. "I feel foolish. I'll change."

"Good idea." All she had to do was get out of that dress and those shoes and everything would be back to normal. He had just breathed a sigh of relief when he heard loud voices, his sister and someone else shouting at each other in Arabic.

Claudia's eyes widened. "Who could it be?" she asked.

"From what I hear, it could only be one person. It's Zahara, and she's very angry."

A moment later a red-faced Zahara stood in the doorway, her hands on her hips, glaring at him. She pointed at Claudia.

"Who is this woman?" she demanded. "Get rid of her immediately or the engagement is off."

Claudia teetered on the strappy high-heeled sandals Amina had given her to try on. She wasn't too steady in these shoes anyway, and with this woman standing there, pointing and glaring at her she was afraid she might just topple over. It was just as she feared, in a matter of seconds, this woman had guessed Claudia was in love with Sam.

But if she was really smart, she'd realize she had nothing to fear from Claudia. Sam would instantly make that clear to her and everyone in the room.

"Zahara, this is Claudia, my American office assistant," Sam said firmly "She works for me. She manages the office. That's all." There, that ought to reassure her. Claudia meant nothing more to him than that. It shouldn't hurt so much to hear him say it, because it was the simple truth. But it did. His words were like a knife through her heart.

Just a glance at the stunningly beautiful woman told her as anything more than words could that Claudia was living in a fantasy world if she thought Sam would ever think of her other than a competent assistant.

"Hah," Zahara said. "I know what I see. I'm not blind. What kind of an assistant appears in a red dress like this? I've never been to America but I know that office personnel do not wear designer gowns. You'll have to come up with a better story than that, Sam."

"It's true," Claudia said. What on earth was wrong with the woman? Wasn't it obvious Claudia didn't fit into the scene here any more than a dandelion fit into a formal garden? No matter what she was wearing she was still way out of their league. She'd never worn a designer gown in her life and if she had a choice she wouldn't be wearing one now. And if she really had a choice, she'd still be back in the office halfway across the world instead of standing here wishing she was invisible.

"I have nothing to do with…anything. I'm here to work, that's all. Really. It's not my dress." She looked at Amina, waiting for her to confirm what she said but Amina seemed more amused than anything and didn't say a word.

Claudia's knees were shaking and she reached down to remove her shoes before she fell over. Was this the kind of family drama they were all accustomed to? If so, she wouldn't last another day in this country.

Sam took Zahara by the arm. "I think it's time

for you and I to have a talk, don't you? It's been a long time. We have so much to say to each other." And he smoothly guided his future bride out of the room.

Claudia turned away so she wouldn't have to see them walk out together, the perfect couple, both tall, good-looking, rich and meant for each other. She picked up the shoes and tried to catch her breath. To hear Sam talk so soothingly to his intended fiancée was painful. Just as painful as she'd imagined back in San Francisco.

Why oh why had she come here? She knew it would hurt. She just hadn't known how excruciating the pain would be. She'd known it was a mistake to get on that plane. Why had she let Sam talk her into it?

"Well," Amina said, her hands on her hips. "That was interesting."

Interesting? That was her idea of interesting? "I hope he'll be able to explain to her," Claudia said. "I wouldn't want to cause any trouble between them." Claudia wished she'd never taken off her old clothes now piled on the chair in the corner.

"I'm afraid you already have," Amina said. "But *tant pis*, as they say in France."

"You heard what she said," Claudia said. "It's

the dress." Claudia cast a rueful glance at the yards of red fabric. "If she'd seen me when I arrived, she'd never have given me a second glance. I can't believe she thinks I'm some sort of a threat to her. It's ridiculous."

"Is it?" Amina murmured. "I wonder."

"Amina," Claudia said as she unzipped the dress and let it fall around her hips to the floor. "Your brother and I work together. I admire him and I think he appreciates the work I do for him. It's the best job I've ever had and he's the best boss in the world." As soon as the words left her mouth Claudia wished she hadn't sounded so adamant. She wouldn't want her words repeated to Sam or anyone however true they were.

"You mean he doesn't make you work overtime, come in early and stay late at the office?"

"Well, yes, sometimes."

"He doesn't call you at home to ask you about work?"

"Of course, but only when it's necessary."

"He's never stubborn or insists he's always right?"

"He usually is right about most things. If he isn't, we talk about it." Claudia could not let his sister make him out to be some sort of ogre. Not that Sam needed her to defend him, it was just that she couldn't help it.

Amina shook her head in mock despair. "I know Sam and I know I couldn't work for him. All I can say is that he's very lucky to have you." She paused and turned her attention back to the clothes, the subject she loved most. Even more than she liked discussing her brother and his overbearing ways. "What is your decision? The champagne peau de soie or the red?"

"You mean the party is on?" Claudia asked.

"Of course. Sam will say all the right things and Zahara will come around. Mark my words. When my brother wants something, he gets it. Surely you've noticed that in the two years you've worked for him?"

"Yes," Claudia admitted, her heart sinking. What she didn't want to admit was that this engagement meant so much to him that he was off sweet-talking his fiancée right now. For one moment her hopes rose thinking that maybe, just maybe the engagement was off. Not that it mattered. He still would never be hers. Now if only she could get out of going to this party. Though there was little hope of that with Amina around.

"What about the black with the bow across

the bodice. That was spectacular on you," Amina said, gathering an armload of dresses to take back with her.

Claudia nodded. She'd tried on so many dresses she couldn't remember which was which. "Fine," she said, feeling as deflated as a hot-air balloon after the party.

"Good choice," Amina congratulated, though actually it was *her* choice. "I'll have my maid run you a hot bath and you can relax until dinner. How does that sound?"

"It sounds wonderful," Claudia said gratefully. Maybe there would be a miracle while she soaked in a perfumed bath. Or maybe by some chance Sam wouldn't be able to convince his fiancée that Claudia was no more important than a fax machine or a scanner. In which case there would be no celebration party. Knowing Sam's powers of persuasion, there wasn't much chance of that.

She was glad for Sam, she really was. Because if you love someone, really love them, you want them to be happy. Why did she think he wouldn't be happy with Zahara? He would. She was perfect for him. Right background, right family, right financial situation. She was everything Claudia wasn't. And Zahara was beautiful, too. He couldn't find anyone who would suit him better.

For his sake, she hoped Amina was right and he'd calm down his fiancée so the engagement would go off as planned. Because she definitely wanted the best for Sam. Why was it so hard to believe that Zahara was really the best for him? He was the only one who could decide that.

CHAPTER FOUR

IF CLAUDIA thought she would be overdressed in the strapless black dress with the bow across the bodice, she was wrong. Every other woman in the richly appointed ballroom with the crystal chandeliers was in a formal gown and every man including Sam was in a tuxedo and black tie or dress robes. The hum of conversations around her were in Arabic, English and a smattering of European languages. There was the scent of expensive fragrances in the air. It was all so sophisticated, she wondered how she'd possibly fit in.

Every man was in formal wear, but no other man looked as dashing and sexy as her boss. Surely she wasn't the only one who noticed. And she did notice. Even though she was taken around the room by Amina and introduced to everyone there, her gaze kept straying across the room and landing on Sam. Once he caught her eye and smiled at her.

She had no idea if it was meant to reassure her or to hide his concern. Maybe it just indicated he thought things were going well. If so she was glad for him. If anyone could reassure a nervous fiancée, it was Sam. She wanted so much to talk to him, to find out exactly what had happened, but Amina was introducing her to friends and relatives and she had no chance to break away.

If Claudia's presence was all Zahara was worried about, then it probably wasn't a big job. But where was Zahara tonight? Why wasn't she hanging on Sam's arm? Why wasn't she accepting best wishes and beaming as a future bride should be? Why was she late for her own party?

There was no reason for Claudia to feel like butterflies were nesting in her stomach. She was just an innocent bystander, no matter what Zahara thought. If Zahara had only caught a glimpse of Claudia's usual self at the office, she'd know she had nothing to fear. Which is probably what Sam had told her. *Claudia works for me. She's a valued and trusted employee. Nothing more.* And she'd believed him. Who wouldn't?

Amina excused herself to greet a man who'd just arrived and was instantly engaged in an animated conversation with him. From the way her eyes were sparkling, Claudia wondered if it was her boyfriend. She wondered what kind of man Amina would be attracted to. Sam's sister looked spectacular in a teal-blue designer dress that showed off her tanned skin to perfection, but when did Amina ever look anything but stunning?

She wasn't beautiful, but with her personality and her sense of style, she would stand out in any crowd. If the man wasn't someone special or even if he was, then Amina was extremely good at flirting, a skill Claudia was lacking. Maybe if she watched and took notes she'd be ready when that tall, handsome stranger appeared in her life.

Standing alone watching the guests, Claudia didn't know anyone she could ask for Zahara's whereabouts. Certainly not Sam. He was far away across the room. But she kept her eyes on the door. It was almost time for dinner and still no Zahara.

"So this is the brilliant assistant Samir has told us about." A man about Sam's age introduced himself as his cousin Ahmad and told her he'd gone to school in the States. "What he didn't tell us was that his assistant was so beautiful."

Claudia smiled at this outrageous compliment. If she looked even close to beautiful, it was thanks to Amina, the makeup she'd applied, the hairstyle she'd had her maid do for Claudia and of course · the black dress.

"Tell me, Sam's assistant," Ahmad said, "what do you think of our little country?"

"I haven't seen much, but I'm sure I'm going to like it," she said politely.

With his hand on her elbow he walked her to the balcony to see views of the spectacular illuminated sculpture gardens below. "It's hard to believe that only forty years ago all that stood here was a stone fort, sand and palm huts," he said, waving his arm toward the city in the distance. "No hotels, no high-rise buildings at all, no fine art, no gardens. I hope your boss is giving you time for some sightseeing while you're here?"

"It depends on how much work we have to do," she said. "But I certainly hope so. I've heard so much about the colorful markets and the camel caravans."

"Have you?" he asked with an amused smile. "Well, if I know Sam he'll be at his desk all day and half the night. And you won't see a thing but what's on the computer screen. The man is a workaholic. Don't look surprised," he said, tilting her chin with his thumb. "You can't work for my cousin and not know that about him."

"Well, yes," she admitted, feeling a little uncomfortable to be touched by a total stranger whose face was only inches from hers. Maybe Ahmad thought all American girls were easy after spending a few years at an American university. "But I'm still hoping to see something of the desert. I've only seen pictures of the dunes and the oases, but…"

"You should see the city from the water. It's the only way to appreciate the spectacular skyline. I have a sailboat and I invite you for a sail. Are you free tomorrow or are you as much of a workaholic as your boss is?"

"No, I mean, I…I really don't know what the schedule is," Claudia said. "I'll have to ask Samir. I assume there will be work to do. That's what I'm here for."

She was here for work, so how could she even consider sailing with a strange man? Surely that's not what she was supposed to do while in Tazzatine.

"Work, work, always work," Ahmad said. "You're only here once. Or maybe not. Maybe you'll like us and our country so much you'll come often." He winked at her.

"There you are," Sam said to Claudia as he came out onto the balcony to join them. "I was looking for you."

"We were just talking about you, Sam," Ahmad

said. "You can't keep this fetching creature holed up in your office all day and night." He gave Claudia's bare shoulder a squeeze. She refrained from stepping backward to escape his touch. No, it wasn't disgust or anger she felt, it was just a slight revulsion. But she was a stranger here and she didn't know what was acceptable behavior and what wasn't.

"It's not right," Ahmad said. "She should at least come sailing with me tomorrow. Say ten o'clock? The winds should be perfect."

Sam looked at Claudia for a long moment, his forehead creased in a frown as if he was asking himself if Claudia had been complaining about him or the work he gave her. The amber lights arched along the ceiling were reflected in his dark eyes. She didn't know what bothered him the most. The idea of her going sailing when she should be working with him or the way she looked tonight. Or maybe something had gone wrong with the engagement. If only Ahmad weren't there, she could ask.

One thing was for sure: Sam must be shocked at the amount of makeup on her face and her new hairstyle, not to mention the black dress. Hopefully he understood this was all his sister's doing and not her idea at all. She'd never even meant to come to this party. But there had been no polite way to get out of it.

"This is a business trip, Ahmad," Sam said shortly. "Claudia knows that. Of course I mean to show her around, but business first."

"He hasn't changed," Ahmad said to Claudia shaking his head in mock despair. Obviously Sam's comments didn't dampen his spirits one bit. "I'll get back to you about this later." With that he bowed slightly and walked away to join a group of young people back in the ballroom.

"In case you're wondering, he hasn't changed, either," Sam said. "The man doesn't know the meaning of hard work. He lives off his inheritance and generally spends his days in leisure. If you want to go sailing with him, by all means go."

"But what about the contract? When do we meet with the Bayadhis?"

"Not until tomorrow afternoon. I was going to…never mind, you should take the opportunity to go sailing. You looked like you were enjoying Ahmad's company. Women generally find him amusing."

From the look on Sam's face, it was clear he found him far from amusing. In fact, downright annoying.

He looked at his watch. There was a long silence while Claudia formed the questions she wanted to ask but was afraid to. Where's Zahara? How did your talk with her go? Is everything okay?

After they'd stood there without speaking for what seemed an eternity, while she waited for him to explain what had happened, Sam stepped back and looked at her. His gaze traveled slowly from her new hairstyle to the tips of the high-heeled sandals she was wearing. His eyes narrowed. She held her breath.

"You look…different," he said at last. No smile. No frown. Just a very intense look directly into her eyes.

She exhaled slowly. What did it mean "different?" Good different or bad different?

"I'm not," she said. "I'm still the same, underneath the clothes and…everything."

"Good," he said brusquely.

Then he suggested they go back inside. "It's almost time for dinner," he said. They both knew no one would sit down to dinner until the guest of honor arrived—the lovely and lucky woman who was getting engaged tonight. Claudia just hoped she could keep her composure when it happened.

"But what about Zahara? Surely we can't start until she arrives."

He didn't say anything. He braced his hands on the ledge of the balcony and stared out into the dark night as if he'd forgotten he'd suggested returning to the ball room. "Of course not," he said at last as if Claudia was crazy to even consider such a thing even though she hadn't.

"Then everything went well? Your meeting with her?" Maybe she was overstepping the bounds between employer and employee, but she couldn't wait another minute to find out.

"Very well. We're in complete agreement, Zahara and I."

Claudia thought she might choke. Complete agreement, he said. How much clearer could it be? How much more did Claudia have to hear before she gave up her crazy dreams? She gave herself a stern lecture. He belonged to Zahara. They were getting engaged. By the end of the night she'd be wearing that beautiful, dazzling five-carat ring Claudia had picked out.

"I'm glad to hear it," she said. "She seemed so upset earlier."

"I know. For some reason she thought you and I were a couple."

"How ridiculous," Claudia murmured.

"That's what I said. Completely. She said she has a sense about these things. She thought I was in love with you."

"*You* were in love with *me?*" Claudia blurted. She wouldn't have been surprised to hear just the opposite, that she was in love with Sam.

He shook his head as if he'd never heard anything so preposterous. "That's what set her off. She's really quite reasonable when you get to know her."

"And beautiful," Claudia couldn't help adding. She didn't say she had no desire to get to know his future bride and to find out just how reasonable she was.

"That, too," Sam agreed.

"Did you get a chance to tell her you didn't believe in love?"

"I didn't think it was the time or place. But I assured her I was not in love with you nor were you in love with me. After all, we work together, that's all."

"So everything is...in order?" Claudia asked.

"Absolutely," he said, turning to go into the ballroom.

Claudia didn't see Zahara come in but the sudden lift of Sam's eyebrows and the half smile on his face told her all she needed to know. He was obviously delighted to see her. And why not? Turning, she saw Zahara looked absolutely gorgeous in a long ivory satin gown that clung to her like it was made for her. Which it was, according to Amina.

No longer angry, she looked serene and calm. Reasonable, Sam had said. An excellent trait for a wife. Heads turned. Of course. Not only was she lovely to look at, but she was the star of the party. She and Sam.

A hush fell over the room as Zahara sailed across the polished marble floor. Claudia would never be able to walk like that in high heels. But Zahara certainly knew how to make an entrance as she came straight over to where Claudia stood with Sam. She kissed him lightly on the cheek and Claudia's heart lurched. How much more could she take? There was not a doubt in anybody's mind these two were meant for each other.

"Did you tell her?" Zahara said to Sam.

"Not yet."

Claudia's gaze moved from Sam's face to Zahara's. Tell her what? She already knew they were about to get engaged. She already figured she'd be let go. She already knew she never should have come here.

"I'm so sorry for this afternoon," Zahara said in a melodic low voice tinged with an intriguing accent. So different from her angry tone a short time ago. "I was not myself. I was worried. I thought…oh never mind what I thought. It was ridiculous. But then we had a little talk and everything is going to be fine now, right, Samir?"

The intimate smile she gave Sam said it all. If they had any problems, they'd solved them. Claudia knew she should be happy for Sam, but she was filled with unbearable feelings of unbecoming envy. How could she help it seeing that Sam and his fiancée had made up and were headed for a happy life together while her life was practically over?

Her job would be finished. She'd go back to California and find another job. But no job would ever compare with this one. No boss could hold a candle to Sam. Why had she ever come here with him? He didn't need her. It was pure torture seeing him with Zahara.

"I'm so happy for you," Claudia said stiffly. As if anyone cared what she thought.

"Thank you," Zahara said. She favored Claudia with a radiant smile.

"I'm sure you'll have a wonderful life together," Claudia added, trying her best to sound sincere. It was the least she could do for Sam.

"I'm sure we will," Zahara said with a glance at Sam who smiled back at her. She was positively beaming now. What had happened during their meeting together? Whatever it was, it had made her very happy. What about Sam? He wasn't the type to smile incessantly. But inside he must be delighted he'd gotten what he wanted. And what he wanted was Zahara. Who wouldn't?

All Sam had to do was assure her that Claudia was no threat to their engagement or their future together. He must have told her she was nothing but a drone, an assistant who worked hard and long but nothing more. He must have painted a rosy picture of their future.

Claudia could see it now. A life divided between two countries. Travel, home, children, financial security and maybe even love. If Sam didn't love Zahara now, he would later. That's how these arranged marriages worked. Divorce was frowned on, so the couples worked out their problems and more often than not, got along just fine. Probably many learned to love each other, which was just a bonus. At least that's how it was supposed to be. If it wasn't, why did it work out so well? With the exception of Sam's parents. But their mistake had been in marrying outside their countries and their cultures. His mother was not from Tazzatine, but Zahara was. They had everything going for them.

When dinner was announced, Sam and Zahara led the parade of guests into the private dining room. Candles gleamed from the tables and the sconces on the wall. White tablecloths, bronze utensils and vases of white roses graced the tables. Sam's cousin Ahmad showed up to escort Claudia. It was better than no one, but it was an effort to smile and make polite conversation with the man. It wasn't his fault. He was outgoing and gregarious; it was her fault for not being able to control her jealousy.

During dinner, over tiny lamb chops, potatoes gratin and petit pois, Ahmad told amusing stories of his and Sam's childhood. Learning to sail on the Gulf, riding horses over the dunes and playing hide-and-seek in the souks. Claudia leaned forward and took it all in. She found their shared past fascinating. Ahmad might be as lazy as Sam said, but he was a great storyteller. While listening, she had no trouble picturing Sam as an adventurous little boy.

But she wondered if Ahmad was right. The Sam she knew really was all work and no play. But maybe if he had someone to take his mind off his work, he wouldn't be that way. Surely Zahara

wouldn't permit him to bury himself in his work
and neglect her. She'd be the type to drag him off
to socialize, which he should do. She hated to
concede that Zahara had any good points, but it
would be good for Sam to get away from the
office. And when she was no longer his assistant,
she wouldn't care what he was doing or where he
was.

It was hard to imagine life without Sam, but it
was about time she forced herself to contemplate
it. In between courses Sam's uncle stood and gave
a short speech about family and love and marriage
and with every word Claudia sank further and
further into depression.

She didn't belong here. She never should have
come. If only she could be swallowed up by the
cold, hard marble on the floor. Instead she had to
sit there, smile, nod and appear interested. Her
head ached from the effort and she just wanted to
go back to the apartment, crawl into bed and
escape this nightmare.

His uncle welcomed Sam back and gave up the
floor to him. Now it was Sam's turn.

"Greetings to all my friends and family," Sam
said smoothly. He looked so happy and relaxed,
Claudia couldn't tear her eyes from him. Even
though she knew what he was going to say. It was

a kind of terrible fixation. Her gaze glued to his, her mind attuned to his. If she had any sense, any willpower, she would have pleaded ill and slipped away now. But she was frozen there, waiting for doom to strike. Waiting for the noose to tighten. Waiting for her life to change forever.

"As you all know, Zahara and I are here tonight to make an announcement that will surprise some but in the end make everyone happy."

Claudia scanned the faces around the tables lighted by flickering candlelight. There was Sam's family at one table. She could be mistaken, but she thought Amina looked puzzled and Sam's father looked positively dour. What was wrong? Would some really be surprised? She thought they'd be ecstatic to see their dreams of uniting the families come true.

"As much as we dislike disappointing our families, Zahara and I have decided to call off our engagement," Sam said bluntly.

Claudia's mouth fell open. Why hadn't he told her? Why had he led her to believe everything was fine? The obvious answer was that he considered his personal life to be none of her business.

The guests around her table gasped in disbelief. More than one said, "Oh, no."

Sam looked around the room as if daring

anyone to challenge him, or even to ask questions. The tone of his voice left no doubt that he was sincere and that the decision was made. The room filled with hushed murmurs of surprise mingled with shock.

When Zahara got up to join Sam at the podium the room fell silent again in anticipation. What could she possibly say? "Thank you all for coming. It is a lovely party. Samir and I are grateful for your understanding and your friendship." Then she walked between the tables, her head held high and left the room.

Now the buzz grew louder, like dozens of disturbed beehives.

"What happened?"

"Who called it off?"

"Zahara."

"What? But whose idea was it really?"

"How terrible for the Al-Hamris."

"I can't believe it."

"What's wrong with her?"

"There's someone else."

"No!"

"Yes."

"What shame on her family."

Claudia sat staring at Sam as he went back to the table where his family was still sitting. The dinner continued. The salad course was next. It consisted of mixed greens, nuts and dried fruit in a lively vinaigrette. But who could taste anything after that stunning announcement? Claudia pushed the lettuce around on her plate.

Ahmad seated at her right appeared unmoved by the whole spectacle and was eating his salad with gusto.

"I knew it wouldn't work," he said smugly. "Never marry a workaholic."

"You mean that's why she's backing out?" Claudia asked, setting her fork down.

"Who says it's her idea?" he asked, sipping his nonalcoholic sparkling beverage. "Maybe Sam realizes he'd make a terrible husband and is doing the poor girl a favor." He made this remark with a knowing smile. "Whatever the reason, you and I are the only ones here who don't appear to be shocked by Sam having the nerve to question his family's wishes. Am I right?"

"I guess so," she said.

"Sam's in big trouble, believe me. His family isn't going to be happy about this."

"Just because he's called off his engagement?" Claudia asked.

"Oh, it's more than that. It's flouting tradition. It's sticking it to your parents. It's like telling them you know more than they do. Not that I don't give Sam credit for standing up for himself. I don't know if I'd have the nerve. You would, wouldn't you?" he asked, leaning toward her.

"I don't know," Claudia murmured. "It's nice if everyone agrees." Maybe if her parents had met Malcolm before the wedding they would have seen something she hadn't and warned her. She kept thinking of Ahmed's remark that Sam would be a *terrible husband*. He was wrong. Sam couldn't be a terrible anything. He was sensitive, kind, supportive…

But what did she know? She'd made a big mistake herself and what had she learned in the mean time? What would she do differently? She'd imagined herself in love. At least Sam and Zahara realized they weren't in love and called it off before it was too late. Or did they? How did it happen? What did it mean? Would Sam eventually tell her?

Waiters circulated bringing the cheese course around to the tables, serving wedges of smooth, a locally made pungent goat cheese, fresh Italian Asiago, a rich Camembert and a tangy blue mottled Roquefort and several other cheeses she'd never seen before with fruit and an assortment of crackers. And after that, coffee and a cake layered with fresh raspberries and whipped cream. If only Claudia could have appreciated it, but her stomach was tied in knots.

Ahmad, her dinner companion, unmoved by the family drama, or just enjoying seeing Sam being the talk of the party, and not in a good way, continued to eat and enjoy the dinner until he'd polished off every last crumb of cake and drunk two cups of coffee.

People were saying goodbye and exchanging hugs and kisses, men as well as women. Clearly the party was winding down. Would it have finished so early if the outcome had been different? Or would they continue to celebrate until late in the evening? Claudia had no idea. Not only was she a stranger in a strange land, but she was also completely unfamiliar with black-tie social events of this kind in her own country. Never mind broken engagement parties.

"What next?" Ahmad said, pulling Claudia's chair out for her. "You haven't had a taste of our nightlife. Let's get out of this gloomy atmosphere. I'll show you a side of the capitol you won't find mentioned in any tourist guide."

"Thank you," she said, eyeing the door with longing. "But I'm very tired."

"Ah, jet lag," he said. "I have a sure cure for it. Partying till dawn."

"I don't think so," Claudia said. All she wanted to do was collapse in Amina's guest room on that divine bed and sleep until the sun shone in on her in the morning. Or until Sam needed her for work. Her feet hurt, her brain was having trouble processing all the events and her face and lips felt too numb to talk anymore.

"Come on, Sam's beautiful assistant," he said, taking her hand and pulling her toward the door.

"No, really…"

"She said no."

Claudia turned to see where the voice had come from and there was Sam on the other side of Ahmad, glaring at him.

"Fine," Ahmad said. "I was just going to see her home."

"I'll do that," Sam said.

Ahmad shrugged. "See you tomorrow then," he said to Claudia. And he went off to party until dawn, leaving her alone with Sam as they made their way to the door. Now was her chance to find out what really happened.

"I don't understand," she said when she couldn't hold the words back another minute. This was not the time to mince words. "If I had something to do with your breaking off your engagement I should know about it."

"You?" Sam said. As if that was the strangest idea he'd ever heard. "Of course not. It's complicated, but that outburst in front of you had nothing to do with you. Zahara was hoping to break off the engagement and was hoping to force the issue by pretending to be outraged by your presence. As if you and I would ever be involved in that way."

Claudia bit her lip to keep from crying. She was tired, drained and ready to fall apart. The disbelief in his voice when he said *you*? had hurt her as much as a slap in the face.

Before she could say another word, his father caught up with them.

"What does this mean?" he demanded, grasping hold of his son. "This is a cruel disappointment to me."

"Father, I'm sorry. I wanted to tell you first. I tried to find you but every time I looked for you you were busy with someone else. In any case I promised Zahara I'd keep it a secret until tonight."

"I don't understand. We've planned this moment for years. Both our families are overjoyed. It is the dream of a lifetime, uniting the families. Everyone is in agreement and then voilà, it's over." His voice shook. "How can this be? You owe me an explanation, son."

Sam nodded and put his hands on his father's shoulders. Claudia looked around for a way to escape this family dispute in which she was an outsider, but she was trapped in the alcove outside the ballroom.

"Zahara is in love with someone else," Sam said. "She called off the engagement. She knows her father will be furious, so I agreed to present a united front to spare her if I could. In any case, after talking with her, I really feel that it's for the best."

"The best?" his father said, his eyes wide with disbelief. "How do you young people know what's best?"

"We can only try," Sam said, "to do what we think is right. This is a big decision. And not an easy one. Zahara will have a battle on her hands."

"Why? What happened? Who is it? Who has taken away my son's fiancée?" he asked. His eyes filled with tears. Claudia felt sorry for the old man. All his hopes dashed by one impulsive almost-fiancée. She was struck by how important tradition was here. How shocking it was for his father to find he'd been disobeyed. And Zahara. What was her father saying to her right now? Knowing it was her decision. Would she be disgraced? Disowned?

Claudia was trying her best to understand a culture where tradition was so important. More important than love or free choice was the respect owed to the older generation.

"The man is someone who works for her family," Sam said quietly.

"A laborer?" his father asked, shocked. "A servant? Oh, this will never do. I feel sorry for the family. What a disgrace. Wicked girl. Disinheritance is too good for her."

"It doesn't matter who he is," Sam said. "All that matters is that she's made her decision which I support."

Claudia wondered how much Sam really supported her decision. Was he hurt? Or was he relieved? Or was he simply caught in the middle, trying to please everyone, trying to make the best of a bad situation? So he wasn't the one who'd called it off. It was Zahara. She'd given up Sam for someone else. Who? Who could possibly compete with Sam for her heart?

"Father, you of all people should understand," Sam said. "You know what it's like to break the rules and marry outside our society."

"Yes, and look what happened. Your mother never fit in. We thought love would be enough. It wasn't. It still isn't. I should have listened to my father. He told me I was making a mistake, but I was young and foolish and refused to be reasonable. I paid the price. And so did you and Amina." Tears formed in his eyes.

Sam patted him on the shoulder. "Don't blame yourself. You provided us with the best of everything. And if you'd married someone else, I wouldn't be here," Sam said with a half smile. "Nor would Amina."

His father shook his head. With a glance at Claudia he said, "This must be your assistant."

"Yes, this is Claudia."

"You must think we are a strange family," he said to her. "An engagement that never takes place. A family torn apart." Just then Amina came rushing up and took in the situation immediately. She put her arms around her father.

"Come, Father, it's time to go home. I have the car waiting. Everything will be fine, you'll see. You'll feel better in the morning." She gave Sam a sharp glance but didn't speak to him. Had she guessed it would never work? Or had she known?

CHAPTER FIVE

As SOON as his father left, Sam led Claudia outside the imposing building. While they waited for the valet to bring his car from the parking garage he paced back and forth, saying nothing. He was so lost in his own world he didn't even seem aware she was there.

Claudia didn't speak, either, not with him in this mood. The look on his face told her he was a thousand miles away. He was obviously upset. But what had upset him? The confrontation with his father or the broken engagement?

"It was hard to hear that my father is sorry he married my mother," Sam said at last, his voice strained.

"Surely that's not what he meant," Claudia said.

"You heard him," he said. "It's enough to discourage anyone from getting married. He said love was not enough."

"He was upset," Claudia said. She had to clench her hands together to keep from smoothing the frown on his brow. "I can't believe he really meant it."

"Oh, he meant it all right," Sam said grimly.

"He was shocked and disappointed, and he was making a point, that's all."

"I know what the point was. He should have been talking to Zahara, not me. He doesn't need to warn me. I'm already convinced. Love and marriage are not for me."

"I think he wants you to get married, but not for love. That's why Zahara seemed like a good choice for you."

"You think I'm a hypocrite, don't you?" he asked, his eyes narrowed. "Knowing how I feel about marriage and love, I was still willing to go through with it."

"It doesn't matter what I think. I don't belong here. I don't understand your customs, but I do understand you felt pressured to do what your family wanted."

"Just so you know, I can't say I'm sorry she called it off," Sam said. "You know me as well as anyone, Claudia, can you really see me married? Tied down? A family man with obligations and a wife who demands I spend time with her instead of at work?" He shuddered as if the very thought was an anathema to him. Then he pinned her with his penetrating gaze, daring her to disagree.

Fortunately the car and driver arrived and she didn't have to answer his question.

In the car, he continued. "You don't have to say anything. I know what your position is."

Claudia turned to him in the backseat, her eyes widened in surprise.

"Love is everything," he said. "Love makes the world go round. Isn't that what you think?"

"Something like that, yes."

"Even after what you've been through?"

"I'd rather not talk about what I've been through. It has nothing to do with your situation."

"Marriage is marriage," he said brusquely. "You called yours off, my fiancée called mine off before it happened. Before things got even more complicated than they were. What happened to you? It might shed some light on the situation."

"I'd rather not," she said stiffly, then turned away and looked out the side window.

There was a long silence as the driver took them down the quiet streets back to the Al-Hamri Building. When Sam finally spoke, he opened a new subject.

"So you're really going sailing with Ahmad?" he asked.

Claudia took a deep breath and tried to act like this was a normal conversation. "I suppose it would be rude to say no. Unless you have work for me to do."

"I'll be meeting with my father in the morning about all kinds of matters that don't concern you. If he's calmed down, that is, and can speak about something besides his supreme disappointment in me. Once we get the broken engagement out of the way we can get back to business."

"Your father was really angry."

"As a foreigner, it must be hard for you to understand."

"I felt sorry for him."

"What about Zahara? Did you feel sorry for her having to marry me when she was in love with someone else? Did you feel sorry that I had to marry anyone when you know my feelings about the institution as a whole? How it goes against everything I believe?"

"Yes," she said, her brain confused and tired. "I mean no. I don't know."

"Of course you don't," Sam said. "You're an outsider. You have no concept of family honor or tradition. Forget I even asked you."

Claudia winced. His words stung.

"As for tomorrow," he continued, "you should take advantage of the opportunity to go sailing and get out on the water." Although the words were encouraging, the look on his face was not. It all boiled down to the fact that he wanted her out of the way while he dealt with his family.

After two years of working for Sam, she could interpret his expressions pretty well. He didn't like the idea of her sailing with his cousin, that was obvious. But he didn't want her hanging around doing nothing. What did he want from her? Ever since they'd arrived in his country, he was not the Sam she used to know. Sure, he was a demanding boss, but she always knew what to expect from him. Not any longer.

The cool air coming from the air-conditioning in the limo was soothing to her flushed skin and her overwrought brain. She didn't want to talk or smile anymore. She simply wanted to close her eyes and forget the problems of the Al-Hamri family.

Why had she come here? She had no role to play, at least not so far. Everything she said was wrong. Everything she suggested was not welcome. She was a fifth wheel, one no one knew exactly what to do with. Send her sailing?

Sightseeing? Dress her up and make her socialize? Fit her into the work schedule whatever that
was?

Sam was sitting so close to her in the wide
backseat the black tuxedo pants brushed against
her bare leg. She shivered. It had nothing to do
with the air-conditioning.

"Your announcement came as a great shock to
your father. Too bad you couldn't have warned
him in advance," she said, even though she knew
he didn't want to talk about it.

"We've been through that, Claudia. Zahara
asked me to keep it a secret and I had to respect
that." He looked out the window and she couldn't
see the expression on his face. She knew he was
relieved more than anything else. He didn't have
to get married. Not now, not ever.

"I hope…I mean, I understand about Zahara
following her heart, but is this really what you
want?"

"How can you ask?" he asked, annoyance in his
voice. "I'm simply not the marrying type. Never
was, never will be. So of course I'm relieved.
Vastly relieved. Father will get over it. He has to."
Sam turned and gave her a tight smile. "Don't let
our family problems interfere with your visit to
our country. They don't concern you. Go sailing.

Try to enjoy the country while you're here. It may be your only chance."

She knew what he meant. This whole trip was such a disaster, he probably wouldn't want to return anytime soon and when he did, he certainly wouldn't bring her.

"Don't you sail?" she asked after a brief silence. If he was brokenhearted, he certainly didn't show it. But knowing him, he wouldn't. If it were her and her engagement had just been terminated, she'd be sobbing hysterically right now.

"I did. My cousin and I took lessons together, along with tennis, golf and skeet shooting. I even had a boat on San Francisco Bay until I found I had no time for it."

Claudia didn't know about the boat. What else didn't she know about him? Plenty, it seemed. "Your cousin thinks you work too hard," Claudia remarked. She'd never uttered a single critical word to Sam in the two years she'd worked for him. She hoped he wouldn't take this as criticism. It didn't come from her.

"And I think he doesn't work hard enough. We're all entitled to our own opinion."

"Maybe the answer is somewhere in between," Claudia suggested. Suddenly she was so tired, she couldn't hold her head up. She lay her head back on the leather seat cushion and closed her eyes.

Back at the Al-Hamri Building, Sam got out first and reached in to help her out. His hand was warm and his grip was firm. His hair had fallen across his forehead giving him that rakish look she loved so much. She was a little unsteady on her spike heels, so she didn't pull her hand from his as she knew she should do.

It was late. She was tired and he must be, too. This was no time to get carried away with the moment. He wasn't getting engaged, but he was still her boss. Nothing more, nothing less. No matter how right it felt to have her hand in his. It wasn't right at all.

No one spoke as they rode up in the elevator, standing so close and yet so far apart. She couldn't think of a single thing to say. If she did say something now, it might be the wrong thing. He'd already as much as told her she didn't understand his family, his country or his situation. He was probably right. On the top floor, he opened the door to Amina's apartment for her.

"I need an aspirin," he said. "I know where she keeps them." He walked down the hall to the bathroom while Claudia collapsed on the big white couch in the living room and took her shoes off.

When he came back he stood across the room on the dark polished teak floor and looked out the window at the twinkling lights reflected in the water. He'd loosened his tie and his expression was unreadable in the dim light from the wall lamp.

"Aside from the surprise announcement and the argument with my father you had to witness, I hope you enjoyed the party," he said.

"It was very nice. I'm not used to such a formal occasion. I wasn't sure what was expected. I hope I didn't make any mistakes. Use the wrong fork or say the wrong thing."

A wry smile touched on the corner of his mouth. "Hardly," he said. "Everyone wanted to know who you were."

"Only because everyone else knew everyone."

"No, because you looked…well, different." He hesitated before the word *different*. As if that wasn't the word he wanted. Maybe he meant outlandish, or bizarre or foreign or out of place.

"I was wearing Amina's dress and shoes." She smoothed the skirt. "I *was* different. Tomorrow I'll be myself again." But she wondered if she'd ever be herself again. Not as long as she was in this strange country.

"Good," he said. "I wish I could believe everyone else will be back to normal, too, but

I'm afraid the whole city will be gossiping about what happened. It's a small country, a small city and a small society. Since our families are prominent in Tazzatine, the whole country will consider it their business, too. There will be gossip, count on it. I'll be blamed."

"Why? You didn't break it off."

"No, but no one knows for sure. You and I know it's because she believes in love and fairy tales and happily ever after."

Claudia smiled. She wanted to shout, *She's right. Love does exist. Whether you want it to or not. Whether it makes sense or not.*

Let him think she was happy for Zahara. When it was her own selfish self she was happy for. "I always enjoy hearing about a happy ending," she said blithely. It was clear Sam's heart was not broken. Even his ego seemed intact.

"A happy ending?" he said with a raised eyebrow. "That unfortunately remains to be seen. She's going to have problems marrying someone so much below her status. But she's a strong-willed woman. I admire that about her."

Claudia felt the air go out of her lungs. How much more did he admire about Zahara? Surely he couldn't be blind to her beauty. Surely the advantages of such a marriage had occurred to him.

Maybe he wasn't as relieved as he claimed. How many times had he used the word? Perhaps he was trying to convince himself as well as her.

She studied his face and tried to remember exactly what he'd said. It was possible he was really disappointed but was covering it up as best he could. And when Sam did his best, it was quite good indeed.

If Claudia thought she could ever match up to Zahara either in looks or willpower, she was wrong. What would she do if she was in love with the wrong man, a man her family didn't approve of? Would she be able to break off an engagement, one that had been in the works for years thus disappointing not one but two prominent families? Fortunately that was not her problem and it never would be.

"It's been a long day," Sam said, running a hand through his hair. "I'm going to bed now and I'd advise you to do the same." He raised his hand in a kind of wave then turned and left.

She watched him close the door behind him and felt terribly let down. For no reason. She'd been to a party. She expected to barely survive the evening but it was over and she had. She'd looked more glamorous than she ever had before or ever would be again and she found out Sam was no longer engaged. She should be happy. Instead she felt like crying. It made no sense at all.

The next morning the maid opened the shutters to a brilliant sunny day. No surprise there. According to her research the country got three hundred plus days of sunshine a year. The maid smiled at Claudia and set a tray on her bed with a glass of fresh squeezed orange juice, a flaky croissant and a large cup of steaming café au lait.

"Miss Amina says to wake you and say you should meet her at the rooftop pool for a swim before it gets too hot."

Before Claudia could protest she hadn't brought a swimsuit with her, the maid opened the closet and brought out several for her to choose from.

There was a maillot, two colorful bikinis and a black racing suit for her to choose from as well as a short white terry-cloth cover-up.

Claudia wanted to ask, But what about work? What about the contract? What am I doing here? I can't spend all day swimming and sailing, can I?

The maid would probably smile and say, why not? But what would Sam say if she asked him? He hadn't seemed at all happy about his cousin's plan to take her sailing. But what did he want her to do?

After she finished her delicious breakfast, she stood on the balcony in the peignoir Amina had given her and took a few pictures of the city below her, the tree-lined boulevards, the steel and glass buildings and the azure sea. She couldn't get over the idea that the new city was transformed from a small settlement of palm huts only a few years ago.

What would happen next to this country? What new buildings, parks, museums and gardens would appear in the next decade? What new industries would appear? What new business opportunities? What new families would emerge? Maybe Zahara would set a new standard by marrying out of her social circle. Whatever happened, Sam's family would be a part of the future.

A swim would feel wonderful. And get her ready for a day of work, not play. After trying on all the suits, and staring at herself in the full-length mirror, she went into a case of shock.

She couldn't wear a bikini. She couldn't even wear a one-piece, high-cut suit. Nor did she feel right dressed like a competitive swimmer. She shook her head and sighed. Then she took a deep breath and put on the bright pink and purple bikini. If she was going to be daring, if she was going to be someone she didn't recognize, why not go all the way? Obviously this was what one wore in the privacy of a private pool, so why fight it? Surely she and Amina would be alone up there.

But they weren't. Sam and Amina were sitting on the edge of the pool, their heads together, their feet dangling in the crystal clear water. The deck was lined with comfortable chaises lounges and umbrellas with striped awnings. Graceful palms fringed the pool and citrus trees in pots, laden with fruit just begging to be picked. Claudia hesitated to interrupt, so she took advantage of the lush foliage to stand in the shade for a moment.

"I knew it," Amina was saying to Sam. "I knew something was wrong all along. Poor Father."

"Thanks for taking him home," Sam said. "I hope he'll come around."

"What else can he do?" Amina asked. "He blames old man Oldalya for not being firm with his daughter. He hopes I won't disappoint the family and run off with one of the servants the way Zahara did."

"Any chance of that?" Sam asked.

"Hardly. It's you he's worried about. He doesn't need to be does he? You're not the type to go falling in love with the wrong woman."

"Falling in love? You know me better than

that," he said. "On the other hand, I'm just as glad to be off the hook."

"You get off scot-free, don't you? Unless you're holding out on me and concealing a broken heart. Come on, aren't you even a little disappointed? Aren't your feelings hurt somewhat? Think of it, she chose a stable hand over you."

Claudia leaned forward to hear his answer. This was just what she wondered. If Sam had any ego, and she knew he had plenty, wouldn't he be just a little bit hurt to be dumped so quickly for someone everyone assumed was his inferior?

His sister softened her remark with a playful slap on his shoulder, then she hopped into the pool and stood waist deep in the turquoise water.

"You think I have no feelings?" he asked.

"You might," she said. "But if you do, they're buried too deep to find them."

Sam, obviously not in the mood for this kind of probing psychology of his innermost thoughts, jumped nimbly to his feet. "Maybe they're at the bottom of the pool," he said lightly. "I'll have a look."

Claudia couldn't tear her gaze from his broad, tanned shoulders, his narrow waist and long legs as he loped toward the diving board. The man had muscles she had only guessed at. She knew he belonged to a gym in San Francisco and that he always made time for a run in the morning in Golden Gate Park, but she'd never seen a physique like his, not even in photographs of famous athletes. Her heart thudded so loudly she was afraid they would hear it.

How anyone in her right mind could turn him down boggled her mind. But then Zahara didn't know him like she did. Didn't know how smart he really was, how insightful and how deep was his appreciation of his country and his family. What a superb companion he could be for the right woman. Whoever she was, it was not Zahara and it was not her.

Others might think they knew him, knew his qualities, but it was only after two years of daily contact with Sam that she really felt she knew him inside and out. And yet…and yet, here he was surprising her by his banter with his sister. It just made her love him more.

For a brief moment the sight of his gorgeous body in his trim swimsuit as he strode across the Moorish tile surface of the pool deck made her feel so light-headed she thought she might pass out before she'd even said hello. She reached for the edge of a sturdy deck chair to steady herself.

She felt a twinge of envy at the siblings' easy

repartee. What if she'd had a sister or brother instead of a lonely childhood as an only child? Amina and Sam didn't see each other very often, but she could see that they'd picked up their close relationship without skipping a beat.

How nice it would be to have someone so close. Someone you knew so well. Someone who shared your background, the memory of a mother who'd left you and a father who could be strict but caring at the same time. Someone to tease and joke with.

She knew Sam had the ability to compartmentalize. So she shouldn't be surprised he could joke with his sister even in the midst of everything that was happening like the merger and the broken engagement.

Sam stepped on the diving board where he tested its springs by jumping up and down.

"See anything?" his sister asked.

"I was right," he said, shading his eyes with one hand. "There they are. My feelings. No wonder I haven't been in touch with them." Then he looked up and cocked his head in her direction. "Claudia?" he said, sounding surprised.

She tried to pretend she'd just arrived and hadn't been eavesdropping on them. She tightened the sash on her cover-up and walked casually toward the pool.

"Come on in," Amina said, waving to her from the shallow end. "You're just in time to race my brother to the end of the pool. He's entirely too arrogant and needs to be beaten."

"I'm afraid I'm not the one to do it," she said.

"Let me see which suit you chose," Amina said.

Claudia took a deep breath and unbelted her robe. She'd come this far, there was no turning back now, no matter how vulnerable she felt. After all, Amina was clad in an even tinier bikini.

"Good choice," Amina said with a smile. "I thought you'd like that one."

Sam lost his balance, tripped and hit the water with a huge splash. Instead of a dive, he'd stumbled and dropped like a stone.

When he came up for air at the end of the pool, he shook the hair out of his face and blinked. Was that Claudia in a bikini? He choked on a mouthful of water. What was happening? First she dazzles his friends and relatives last night and today she shows up in a bikini. This was all Amina's doing and she had to stop. Claudia was his assistant. She was going sailing with his cousin today. It was getting hard for him to know where she fit in anymore.

"Where did that come from?" he demanded of his sister in a low voice. First the dress, now this. How many more shocks could he take?

"I assume you're referring to the swimsuit," Amina said. "It's part of a new line I'm carrying. You can't imagine how popular they are. I can hardly keep them in stock. Women come to Tazzatine because it's a shopper's paradise. They get to buy the most fabulous clothes and naturally wear them. Not that bikinis are worn on the public beaches, of course not. But in hotels and private pools, why not?"

Why not? Sam asked himself. On anybody but Claudia he couldn't object. But seeing her in nothing but a few scraps of cloth made him extremely uncomfortable. He tried to look away but he couldn't.

"I think she looks great, don't you?" Amina asked just as Claudia walked to the deep end and slipped into the water.

"You don't understand, Amina, Claudia is here to work with me."

"I understand that you work way too hard and so does she. She probably never complains but she should. You're not in California now. You may have forgotten, but we have a different life-style here. We take time to enjoy life. Don't tell me you don't need a break. You already look better than when you arrived."

He shook his head at his sister. As if it would do any good. She'd always had a mind of her own and she still did. While they were talking, Claudia seemed intent on getting exercise by swimming energetically back and forth and he was spared from staring at the shapely body he had never known existed under her work clothes. How did she feel about exposing so much skin in broad daylight? He couldn't ask. It was none of his business.

"If you don't have anything to do, you should take Claudia sightseeing."

"I'm afraid she's busy and I'm meeting with Father," he said, admiring her neat strokes out of the corner of his eye. "Ahmad is taking her sailing."

"I didn't know that," Amina said with a frown. "Why didn't someone warn her? He'll flirt with her and talk her arm off. I'm sure you could get her out of it if you wanted to. Tell Father you're busy, say you need her because you have work to do, but then change your mind."

"I can't do that. You know you're just as devious as ever. Did it occur to you that maybe she wants to go?" It had certainly occurred to him. Ahmad could be charming and fun, so he'd been told. "You're the one who says we should all relax and have fun," he told his sister.

"That means you, too. Take Claudia to walk the corniche, to see the old fishing village and the craft shops. She'll have much more fun with you than Ahmad."

"I'm not sure about that. I can't spend half the day just wandering around the city like a tourist."

"Why not? You might have a good time. You never know."

When Claudia came up for air, he asked her what she wanted to do today.

"I'm here to work," she said. He was glad to hear her say it. But maybe she wanted to go sailing instead of working and she was afraid to admit it thinking it wasn't appropriate. Maybe she found Ahmad amusing. The water dripped off her hair onto her bare shoulders and the top of her bikini just covered her breasts.

Again he tried to look away but it was impossible. The whole scene was so strange he wondered if he was dreaming. This was not the way he pictured this trip at all. His engagement was off. He'd barely recovered from that shock when his assistant had shown up at his pool half naked, which had him reeling.

"You heard her," he said to his sister. "She feels the same as I do. We're not here to play." If only Claudia would get back into her old clothes, then everything would return to normal and he could concentrate on business. But the world seemed determined to thwart him at every turn. He had more control over events back at the office in San Francisco.

His trusted valet was at the edge of the pool gesturing to him. What now? He braced his arms on the tiles, and pulled himself out of the water.

"Sorry to bother you, sir," Karim said, "but your father called on urgent business." He handed Sam the phone. A minute later his father was on the line.

"There's been a delay with the merger. Old man Bayadhi is in the hospital. Not sure what it is. Maybe a heart attack. Did you notice last night? He hasn't looked well."

"What does this mean?" Sam asked.

"I don't know." His father sounded tired. "I've had enough of these ups and downs. I'm going to concentrate on something else for a change and I need your help."

"Of course," Sam said. As long as it didn't have to do with the canceled engagement, Sam would agree to anything.

"I have my eye on a prize camel I hear is for

sale this week. If I felt better I'd head off to Sidi Bou Said and from there on to the camel market."

"Shall I go for you?" The idea was appealing. Sam was tired of the ups and downs as well. "It may not be bad strategy to pull back for a while. Let Bayadhi recover if that's what he needs and let them think we're not all that eager for the merger."

"I knew you'd agree," his father said. "The old coot may have a dozen more objections to the agreement. I hear he's sent me a list of changes he wants made. I haven't seen it. I wouldn't be surprised if he's out for a week or more. He may be faking it just to put off the merger. To try to get more out of us. As for me, I don't feel like traveling just now. Take your secretary with you, maybe get some work done. But don't fail to come back with my camel. I've called ahead, the house will be in order."

"A week or more?" Sam said. He'd thought longingly about Sidi Bou Said, his horses, the family house, the dunes and the desert, but how could they justify taking off for a week's vacation unless he really could get something done there. With Claudia along it made sense. They could go over the contract there just as well as here.

"Your secretary should see something of the country before she leaves. Otherwise she'll believe

Tazzatine is all five-course meals, glass houses and high-rise office buildings being constructed."

"Fine," Sam said. "We'll be ready to go in an hour."

Claudia got out of the water and wrapped herself in her terry robe, which made it much easier for Sam to explain the change of plans. Of course he couldn't tell her what to wear, especially with his sister around filling her head with fortune tellers and emptying her closet to dress her as if she were a doll.

"The old man is sick?" Amina said. "That's just what Durrah predicted. Maybe now you'll believe in her." Amina looked at Sam then at Claudia. "And that's not all. That tall, dark stranger in her future? It could be Ahmad."

Sam shook his head. "Since she's already met him, how could he be a stranger? Amina, forget the fortune teller. Claudia is far too sensible to believe in that nonsense."

"Yes, Sam, we know your feelings on the subject. In any case, I'm staying in town," Amina said, "but Claudia must go with you to see the desert."

"That's what Father said," Sam said. He turned to Claudia. "I'm afraid you'll miss your sailing date."

"I don't mind," she said.

"Then it's settled, Amina will let Ahmad know your change of plans. The Bayadhis are sending over a list of changes to the contract. We can just as easily work on them at the villa. Better perhaps, without any interruptions."

Amina sent a knowing look in her brother's direction. *See,* her look said. *It's all working out for the best.*

CHAPTER SIX

CLAUDIA would have been ready immediately, but Amina insisted on packing a suitcase for her and filling it with clothes she didn't know she'd need. But Amina was probably right. She knew what life at the family compound was like and Claudia didn't. She was happily raiding her closet for riding clothes, loose cool robes, shorts, tank tops and sandals and light cotton sleepwear. And of course two swimsuits to choose from.

Once the car was filled with the luggage, Claudia, Sam and the chauffeur, they headed out of town on a six-lane super-highway.

They passed a large billboard with a picture of a fatherly figure in a white djellaba and some Arabic script written above it.

"My uncle," Sam explained. "His Highness Sheikh Mohammed Ben Ali Maktoum. You were asking what an emir is? He was one, and a fine one.

He died a few years ago but he's still much admired."

"What does it say?"

"It's a proverb. 'If you have much, give of your wealth. If you have little, give of yourself.'"

"Which did he give?"

"Both. He ruled with honor and established a foundation with his money."

"Will that be you someday?"

"With my face on a billboard? I don't think so. I wouldn't want to scare the wildlife or small children," he teased.

Claudia smiled. She could just see Sam's gorgeous face smiling down on the admiring populace. "What I mean is will you rule the country someday like he did?"

Sam shrugged. "It's possible. But I'm afraid I don't have his political savvy. Besides he married into a prominent family and united the country." He slanted a glance at Claudia. "I know what you're thinking. If I'd married Zahara…"

"Well?"

"No," he said, hitting the seat cushion with his fist for emphasis.

Claudia's eyes widened. She gripped the edge of the seat.

"How many times do I have to tell you how

happy I am, how relieved I am that I'm not getting married. To anyone. I realize now what a huge mistake it would have been. I plan to celebrate my freedom every day from now on. What more can I say besides marriage, commitment and fidelity are all out of the question. No merger, no family pressure, no inheritance, no power is worth it."

"I see," Claudia said. Only a fool would fail to see. That's how clear he'd made himself. "Anyway, your uncle sounds like a wise man."

"He was. We miss him. The whole country misses him. He had many other wise sayings, which have been collected and published." He looked at his watch. "This is turning out to be an entirely different trip than I imagined. I hope you're not bored."

"Hardly. I'm supposed to be working, instead I'm having a paid vacation, seeing things I never expected to see in my life. It may be old to you, but to me everything here is new and fascinating."

"I'm glad you came," he said soberly. "Seeing the country through your eyes has given me a fresh point of view and clarified a few things for me."

He didn't say what things, but she wondered. Did he think of returning to live here for good? Did he wonder what would happen when his father died? Would he then take over for him?

Maybe he wouldn't make an advantageous marriage and unite his country, but he could still do some very useful things.

Soon the road dropped down to two lanes and began winding into bare lunar mountains.

"Sandstone," Sam said, with a gesture toward the cliffs in the distance. "Once we cross the mountains, we're in pure desert."

He was right. They left the mountains behind and as far as she could see, the road stretched straight as a ruler across the sand. How far was it to their oasis at Sidi Bou Said?

"Those are Bedouins," Sam said, pointing to men in hooded shirts herding goats along the side of the road. "The nomadic ones who control the desert. They know where the water sources are."

"Isn't it hot for them to live out there?"

"They're used to it and if they need to, they can take refuge in the rocky ravines. They carry their tents of goat or camel hair with them. It's been their way of life for centuries. They prefer the nomadic life."

"I can understand their wanting to live on their own, away from the crowded city."

"How so?" he asked, slanting a curious glance at her as a huge truck carrying drilling equipment passed them. "You're a city girl, aren't you?"

"Yes, and I love my place in San Francisco…it's close to everything. Museums, parks, coffee shops. But if I were a Bedouin I'd want space to breathe. No cement, no tall buildings blocking the light."

"How would you like living in a tent?"

"I don't know. I've never been camping."

"Look over there," Sam said. "The oil derricks always remind me how much the country has changed." He pointed to a series of pumps on the horizon.

"Life at Sidi Bou Said is far from camping," he said. "Wait till you see the compound. You'll understand why my father likes to get away to it as often as possible."

"What about you?"

"I'm glad he suggested it. It's been a long time since I've been there. It's a good place to unwind. Maybe that's why Father suggested we go. But of course the whole reason he wants me here is to attend the camel market and buy one for him."

Claudia didn't think Sam looked like he needed to unwind. He looked relaxed and Westernized in his casual khaki slacks and knit shirt. He looked like he would be at home anywhere. Paris, London, New York, Tazzatine and of course, San Francisco.

"But is it home to you?" she asked.

"I don't know if I have a home." One corner of his mouth quirked in a half smile, but he sounded a little sad.

Though he didn't know if he had a home, Claudia tried to picture him at home in traditional robes here in his country. Maybe he never wore them. She kept thinking of how he looked in his swimsuit and she wondered if they'd be swimming at the compound. She hoped not.

If she had another view of Sam's half bare body, his smooth tanned skin, broad shoulders and his damp hair slicked back from his face, she didn't know how she was going to keep her lust for him under control. It was one thing to work side by side with him and quite another to take a quasivacation with him.

She acknowledged once again she shouldn't have come on this trip. No matter how fascinating or mind-altering. It was turning out worse for her self-control than she imagined. First dealing with the fact he had a fiancée. Then the cancellation of the engagement. Then the fortune teller and the swimming pool. And now this trip out of the city. Who knew what further temptations and disappointments she'd have to endure?

"Who will be at the compound?" she asked.

Hopefully many other guests and distractions so she wouldn't be on her own with Sam.

"Just us and the servants. It won't be very exciting. First I spoiled your sailing date and now I've abducted you to an oasis so I can buy a camel for my father. Hardly what you expected, is it?" He gave her a half smile that made her wish he'd smile at her more often. But if he did, how would she get through the next few days without falling even more hopelessly in love with him?

Her goal was to avoid situations that led to any kind of intimacy, and if she did, she might come out of this alive. She told herself things would be better when they were actually doing work. But when was that going to happen? When would they sit down and go over these changes he'd mentioned? What if the situation changed while they were off in the desert? Just the two of them. She pressed her thumbs against her temples in an effort to rid herself of the impossible dreams that threatened to crowd out reality.

"Anything wrong?" Sam asked.

She dropped her hands. "Oh, no, just a little headache." And a little heartache, which is worse. Much worse.

He reached into his briefcase and took out a small bottle of pills. He shook two out and handed them to her, brushing her palm with his fingers. Then he gave her a bottle of chilled water from an ice chest behind them.

She swallowed the pills and wondered how it was possible for him to be so thoughtful. A man who'd been waited on all his life still knew how to make someone like her feel better.

She wondered how he really felt. Was he tired of the city, tired of dealing with a broken engagement, his sister and high society, tired of playing tour guide for her? If he was frustrated by the delay in negotiations, he didn't let any of it show. She knew he was good at riding the ups and downs of business; she didn't know how he'd handle disappointments of a personal kind.

A short time later, Sam told the driver to pull off the road to stop for tea next to an encampment of nomads. Before the servants could build a fire to heat the water, the chief of the Bedouins had spread out hand-woven carpets for them to sit on, brewed a pot of mint tea and passed a basket of fresh dates for the guests.

"So this is the desert hospitality you've told me about," Claudia murmured to Sam who was sitting next to her.

Sam nodded. "They're poor and they don't know us but we are welcome to share what they have."

"Would they mind if I took their pictures?" she asked.

After negotiating and slipping coins into their host's palm, Claudia photographed Sam and their hosts.

Then she sipped her tea thoughtfully while Sam and the desert men engaged in an animated discussion. It could have been about the price of goats or oil production, she had no idea.

"I can't imagine this happening anywhere else in the world," she said to Sam. "Stopping by the side of the road and having people make tea for strangers. It's a wonderful custom."

Sam put his hand on her bare arm. And suddenly her temperature rose. Her face flamed and she couldn't catch her breath. "I'm glad you appreciate it," he said. "It takes a stranger to see our country the way you do. I take these things for granted. I shouldn't."

She was a good swimmer. She'd proved that to herself and anyone else who noticed this morning. But when she looked into his deep, dark eyes she knew what it was like to be in danger of drowning. She tried to take a deep breath, but her heart was racing.

"Are you sure you're okay?" he asked. "You're not having a heat stroke?"

"Oh, uh, maybe I did get too warm."

He frowned. "This is my fault for dragging you out here and making you drink hot tea. I wanted you to have the Bedouin experience. But it's too warm. We'd better get you back to the air-conditioned car." He helped her to her feet, took her hand and led her back to the car.

Claudia should have protested. She should have said she was fine, just a touch of heartache, but of course she didn't. She just let herself give in to being taken care of for a moment. She let him worry about her and hold her hand all the way back to the car. She should be ashamed, but she wasn't. Back in the car, she closed her eyes and let the cool air wash over her while she gave herself a stern lecture.

He's not for you. If you don't know it now, you're hopeless and there's something seriously wrong with you. It's not heat stroke and it's not a broken heart. It's pure runaway imagination. And some kind of dumb hope in the impossible. Just because he doesn't have a fiancée and doesn't want one, doesn't mean he wants or needs someone to love or to love him. He's the most independent, self-sufficient man in the world. Remember you've already suffered a broken heart. You don't need to put yourself through that again.

What she needed was a good, strong dose of reality. No doubt it would be delivered when she needed it most.

But reality was not to be found at the house in the Palmerie. Everything about it was magical, something which was apparent from the moment they entered the stone gates of the villa. After the heat of the unrelenting desert, they were suddenly in a cool, green grove of palm trees where a group of servants stood waving and waiting for them. Flanking the entrance were two ancient cypress trees soaring to the sky, and just inside a huge bright magenta colored bougainvillea covered a pergola.

"It's beautiful," Claudia murmured. It was more than beautiful. It was enchanting. Like something out of a fairy tale.

"I'm glad you like it," Sam said. "Come. I'll show you around. If you're not too tired."

"Oh, no. Not at all."

As they walked, she breathed in the sweet scent of orange blossoms. To one side of the house was the Moorish tiled swimming pool where a Carerra marble fountain sent a stream of water splashing into it.

"I hope you brought your suit," he said.

She sighed. "Yes, Amina packed for me." She

could only hope Sam would be too busy for any swimming.

"Then she's thought of everything," he said.

Everything but the fact that Claudia was in love with her brother. She couldn't have thought of that.

"On the other side of the garden is the guest cottage. It's where my parents spent their honeymoon. If you like you can stay there, though I thought you'd prefer a room on the second floor of the main house."

"Of course. The main house is fine."

"You look like you've recovered completely from the heat," he said, studying her face.

"Who wouldn't recover in this lovely place," she said, tucking a strand of hair behind her ear. Though she'd never worn her hair down to the office, Amina had braided it for her before they left today, and she felt young and cool and free in a way she had never felt before. Sam probably wouldn't have noticed if she'd had it cut in a Mohawk. "I wouldn't have missed the tea for anything."

"You have to watch out for the sun. It's quite intense. Here in the Palmerie at least we have shade."

"It's like something out of the *Arabian Nights*,"

she said, gazing around in rapture at the sight of orange, lemon and apricot trees loaded with fruit. The sky above them was the most intense blue she'd ever seen.

"The nights are beautiful here, too. You can see more stars than any place else I know. No city lights to interfere." He looked around as if seeing it for the first time.

"How long has it been since you were here?" she asked.

"Too long. I'm glad it worked out this way. Father was right. Coming here now was the right thing to do. Thanks for being so flexible. That's what I've always appreciated about you."

She managed a small smile. He appreciated her flexibility. It was better than nothing. She was a fool if she thought he'd appreciate anything else like her new clothes or her hairstyle. Oh, yes, he did appreciate her brain and her talent for analyzing contracts. That should be some comfort to her.

"Now for the house," he said, leading the way to the arched front entrance. "Long ago Father remodeled it in traditional Arabian style thinking my mother would appreciate it. It has three main areas—the large living room, a dining area and a master bedroom."

Hearing that made Claudia wonder how his mother could ever have left this beautiful place. Homesickness must have been a terrible affliction for her. The main living area had a hand-made marble floor surface called Tadelakt and portraits on the wall that had belonged to Sam's grandfather.

"It's like an art gallery," she said, gazing up at the pictures on the rough-surfaced wall. "Is it all right if I take photographs of them?"

"Of course. Of anything you like."

Her fingers itched to get her camera out and visit the grounds quietly on her own, taking pictures so she'd never forget this house and grounds.

Before they could tour the compound, the servants appeared with trays and motioned for them to come onto the terrace for refreshments. They sat under a tented canopy surrounded by lush greenery and drank fresh, cold lemonade squeezed from fruit from their own trees and ate small, hot flaky spinach turnovers. On the table were bowls of pine nuts, almonds and pistachios.

"Where's the office?" Claudia asked, after quenching her thirst with the tart lemonade.

"In the other wing of the house. I'll take you there next. I'm glad Amina or cousin Ahmad aren't here—they'd say you're as bad as I am, looking for work before you've even unpacked."

"But that's what I'm here for. That's why I came. I'm here to help you."

"You are helping me. You're helping me see things the way they are. If you weren't here I wouldn't appreciate this place the way I should. I wouldn't see my cousin for who he is or realize that I'm better off without Zahara, no matter how right it seemed at the time."

"I made you realize that?" she asked, her voice so high it was almost a squeak. "I never said a word."

"You didn't have to. All I have to do is look at your face and I know what you're thinking."

Claudia pressed her lips together and looked away. It couldn't be true. If it was, he'd know how she felt about him, and he didn't. He couldn't.

He reached across the table and took her hand in his. Her heart thumped loudly. Claudia wondered if she was dreaming.

"Don't ever play poker," he said, tilting his head to give her a long look. "You'd never be able to hide your hand from your opponent."

Was she dreaming or was this Sam sitting across the table, holding her hand and teasing her. She'd known him for two years, and yet she'd never seen this side of him. Maybe no one had except his sister.

If he only knew how good she was at concealing her feelings for him, he wouldn't say that.

He turned her hand over in his and traced a line in her palm with his finger. Goose bumps ran up and down her arm. "So what did the old girl have to say when she read your palm?" he asked. "Besides the part about the tall, dark stranger."

"Oh, just the usual," Claudia said. But she was so unnerved by the touch of his hand on hers she couldn't remember what Dhurra had said at all. "Um, long, happy life. That kind of thing."

"I'll tell you what I see," he said. His thumb was making circular motions on her palm making her unable to say another word or even think straight.

Claudia leaned forward. She should take her hand back. She should stand up. She should get to work. Go to her room. Unpack. She should do anything but sit here as if he'd cast a spell over her. Or maybe it was the oasis that had done it. But she didn't move. She couldn't.

"This, of course is your fate line," he said. He looked up and met her gaze.

"How do you know?"

"When we were small Amina and I had a nanny

who was an expert. She had her book of palms, which she studied. It had pictures of all these lines. She told Amina she would wear beautiful clothes and that I would follow Father into business." He smiled as if they were both in on a little joke.

"I know you and I know you're skeptical of these seers. And yet you have to admit she was right."

"Because she predicted the obvious. Amina has always loved dressing up and my destiny was to follow in Father's footsteps. Nothing magic about that. But at the time we were impressed. We were young and we thought she was not only old but very wise. She used to say fate controls your life. I don't believe it anymore, but let's just see if I remember what the fate line reveals." Again his fingers began sensuously tracing the lines of her palm.

Claudia's throat was clogged, her vocal chords had shut down. His hand that held hers was firm and strong.

"Ah, here it is. The angle of the line says that you surrender your interests to those of others like myself. That's why we work so well together. You give your all to me and the job, don't you?" He looked up to meet her gaze and held it for a long moment. She didn't know how to answer so she just shrugged.

"If I remember right this is the marriage line," he said, turning back to look at her palm. His thumb moved to stroke the most sensitive part of her palm. She felt her heart melt as if she'd left it out in the desert sun.

"Very interesting. You have more than one line. More than one marriage. This is the first." He held up her hand to show her. "And this is the second. The lines that meet the marriage line but don't cross it mean children, four children."

"Stop," Claudia said. "I have no plans to ever remarry and I don't plan on any children. This is complete nonsense. You don't believe it any more than I do." She snatched her hand back.

"Maybe I was wrong," he said. "Maybe there's something to it after all. You've been married, that's marriage number one."

"I thought you were going to show me your office," she said, getting to her feet. She was feeling desperate to get this trip back on kilter. "I thought we had work to do."

"That was before I saw your hand," he said with a roguish smile. "But if you insist. I'll have to tell Amina that you're a bigger workaholic than I am. Is that what you want? Very well. Come with me."

He stood and stretched, giving her a tantalizing glimpse of his flat tanned stomach. "It's a complete office, though maybe it shouldn't be. Father and Amina hate it when I go in and close the office door. They insist this house should be for rest and relaxation. Maybe when I'm older I'll agree. In the meantime we'll have a look at the papers Father gave me and decide if the changes are reasonable. Then we'll check in with our office back home."

"Home?"

"I meant San Francisco. Frankly I don't know where home is. Maybe it's here." He paused and looked around at the trees, the brilliant flowers and the bubbling fountains that sent water cascading from a brass pipe. He took Claudia's arm and looked at her so intently she didn't know what to expect. "I envy you, Claudia, you have a home in a city you can go back to. You know exactly where you belong."

"But you're at home in many places. Here, in the city, in the States or wherever you are."

"Could you be at home here?" he asked suddenly. His gaze didn't waver, as if her answer was important to him.

"I...I don't know. It's a beautiful place, but it doesn't feel real to me. It's like a dream."

He nodded and dropped her arm. "Let's get some work done," he said. He was suddenly all business. As if they'd never left San Francisco. As if he'd never seen her in a cocktail dress or a bikini. As if he'd never read her palm. Then they went to his office, which was cool and air-conditioned. He spread out the contract with the changes pencilled in. "See what you make of it," he said. "While I check in with our office."

Claudia immediately zoned in on the pages in front of her, writing comments in the margins. She was aware that he'd switched on his computer and read his messages. When she finally looked up she noticed he was leaning back in his chair, watching her.

"What do you think?" he asked.

"There are a few problems. I have some ideas. Let me go through the whole thing first, then we can talk about it. See if you agree with me."

He nodded, but he continued to stare at her.

"What's wrong?" she asked.

"I don't know. Maybe it's all that talk about my being a workaholic. Maybe it's this place, but I can't concentrate. I've always appreciated you, Claudia, but I didn't realize how much I depend on you until now."

Claudia shifted in her chair and turned back to

the contract. He made her nervous, looking at her like that. He wasn't himself and she thought she knew why. Say what he would, he was upset by his broken engagement.

Finally he picked up the phone and called his father. Claudia didn't know if she was supposed to listen, but she did. It sounded like the merger was still in limbo. After he hung up, she talked about the contract with him and suggested several ways they could get things moving again, such as some incentives for the Bayadhis to participate.

"We should remind the Bayadhis of the advantages of the merger. Perhaps they're not aware Al-Hamri Shipping has just taken delivery of four new bulk carriers. We know they have a contract with Australia to ship ore to China. How will they get it there without our carriers? As far as we know, leasing is not an option for them right now."

"Brilliant," Sam said. "I'll call Father back."

"Wait. Let's come up with some more advantages for them."

They spent an hour tossing ideas back and forth just as they always did, then Sam called his father back. She heard him giving her full credit for most of the suggestions. It gave her a warm glow hearing him speak. Sam was never one to take credit for anything she'd thought up.

"Father was impressed," Sam said. "But we won't really know if it worked until the agreement is signed. In any case, you've earned your salary this month," he said. "In fact, I think you deserve a raise."

"Sam, you just gave me a raise last month," she protested with a blush.

"Which you deserved as well," he said. He stood and walked around the room, looking at the pictures on the wall, the plaques and the awards and the trophies as if he'd never seen them before.

"Time for a break," he announced. "That's enough for today. You haven't seen your room yet. Amina would never forgive me if she knew I'd taken you to the office first."

She followed Sam up the stairs where he left her alone in the guest room that was decorated in warm yellow and cool blue tiles. She found the servants had unpacked for her so she changed into cropped pants and a short-sleeved T-shirt, which were both a little snugger than what she usually wore. They were Amina's and though Amina and she were about the same size, Sam's sister wore her clothes tighter than Claudia did. Of course Amina's wardrobe was totally different from Claudia's, which was part of the reason Claudia was having a hard time figuring out who she really was.

She took her camera and climbed up the steps to the roof garden that overlooked the palm forest. There she snapped picture after picture. When she got home she'd print them out and make a montage for her wall. It would remind her of this amazing place that she'd never see again. Her memories would be bittersweet. The engagement, then the breakup. The party, then the solitude of this desert refuge. The luxury, the servants, the kindness of Sam's family.

The silence of the palmerie was broken only by the palm fronds whistling in the soft breeze and the chirping of the brightly colored birds that flitted from tree to tree.

For the first time today she was able to completely relax. She knew she needed a break from Sam. Every day, every hour and every minute spent in his company brought her closer and closer to the one man she could never have. She had to constantly be on guard, afraid she'd say something that would enable him to guess how she felt about him. Every time he looked into her eyes, held her hand, read her palm, or exchanged ideas made her wonder if one of these times she'd slip and confess.

If this trip to his homeland had showed her

anything, it was that she was an outsider. One thing after another. The reaction of his father to the broken engagement. The importance of family. The possibility of Sam's picture appearing on billboards as the benevolent sheikh. She would never ever fit in. That's why she came here, she reminded herself. For a reality check. Well, she was getting it.

In their office in San Francisco it was easy to forget he was a sheikh and she was a commoner from another country. There he was just another executive and she was his trusted assistant. They worked together and that was all. But here the lines were blurred between work and play. It didn't seem to bother him, but it disturbed her. It made her discontented. It made her want more. It made her into a different person.

Sam might not feel the same, but he most likely needed a break from her, too. It must be tiring to always be explaining, translating and showing her around. He'd just said he was tired of working. As for her it was tiring to be on her guard all the time, afraid to let her feelings show. She couldn't imagine anything worse than raising his suspicions and feeling his pity for his poor, deluded assistant who couldn't control herself.

* * *

Sam went to his room on the second floor and changed into cargo shorts, leather sandals and a T-shirt. He could go back to the office and do some more work, but he didn't really want to be dragged back into work today. Not without Claudia, and he'd already taken too much of her time. For the first time in months he felt like stepping back from the problems of shipping lanes, contracts, revenues, and this merger. He never took vacations. Never felt the need.

It must be the oasis. He hadn't been here for a long time. It was having a strange effect on him today. Maybe it was the influence of his father who always loved this place above all others. Maybe it was because his mother had felt more at home here, though not enough to stay.

Why hadn't his father known that before he married her? As Claudia said, it was not reality. It was like a dream. Of course she couldn't live here. She was an outsider just like his mother.

Having Claudia here and seeing it through her eyes made him see the place as he'd never seen it before. As his mother must have seen it. It was a beautiful oasis, but it was not home. The look on her face as they drove through the gates said it all. She'd fallen under its spell, too. But for how long? After a few days most visitors got restless.

Some found it isolated. Some too rustic. Some too hot. Those who were vulnerable to its charm loved it for the gardens, the pool, the fountain and the trees and most of all, the solitude. Claudia seemed to appreciate it all. He couldn't get over how she'd changed.

His usually stiff and proper assistant had looked positively dreamy-eyed when he showed her around. He had a picture in his mind of Claudia picking a yellow hibiscus flower from a vine and stopping to listen to a songbird.

But what if she knew this was her home and she couldn't leave. What then? He knew the answer. He'd seen it all happen to his mother. First the romance, the excitement, the thrill of a different country. Then reality hit, family pressures, different customs, the longing for home and she had to leave. His father had never gotten over her departure.

Was it true Sam was a workaholic and now he was paying the price? Was it that he was married to his work the real reason why Zahara wouldn't marry him? Or did she really believe she'd found true love with the family groom? Why else would she risk her family's disapproval by making such a drastic decision that would affect the rest of her life? Not just hers, but her family's as well.

He had to admire someone who'd take a risk like that. Even though he didn't believe in love, Zahara obviously did. Every woman he knew did. Take Claudia. She'd been in love and had married the man. Then she got a divorce. Her marriage line said she'd marry again. She should. She'd make some lucky man very happy.

He didn't go back to the office. He'd wait to hear from his father and he and Claudia would go back to work together. Here in the desert he would let the warm air wash over him like the wind blew across the dunes and shaped them into lush curves of golden sand.

He looked up and there was Claudia on the balcony above him with her camera held out in front of her. It had to be Claudia, and yet he scarcely recognized her. She not only looked like a different person, but she acted like a different person, too.

As long as he'd known her, he had no idea she was interested in photography. He had no idea what she was interested in at all. He'd just found out about her knitting and her book club. From where he stood he could see her face was flushed and her hair had escaped the braid she was wearing and framed her face in soft tendrils.

Was this the same woman who sat at a desk all day in her office in San Francisco? She was so involved in her picture taking, she didn't see him down there, so he continued to stare at her and wonder at the change in her. Or was he the one who'd changed?

"Come down," he called to her when he was no longer content to just look at her.

She looked down from the balcony and nodded.

He found he was impatient for her company. She hadn't seen all of the place yet. Showing her around was more fun than he'd had for months. She appreciated everything he offered, from food to flowers, to birds and fruit, to people and the pictures on the wall. Now he wanted to see what she'd think of his prized possessions.

"Hurry. I have something to show you."

CHAPTER SEVEN

"WHAT is it?" she asked when she joined him on the terrace.

He was distracted to see her once again in casual clothes. Different clothes from those she wore this morning. Her shirt and pants hugged her body giving him yet another opportunity to see that she did indeed have curves. Well, what did he expect? She was a woman. They weren't in an office. She could wear whatever she wanted.

When he didn't answer she followed up with another question. "Any more news from the office?"

"Nothing," he said. "It's too soon." He didn't tell her he hadn't even checked and didn't want to. "I'm going to go see my horses. I thought you'd like to see them, too."

"I would," she said, her eyes lighting up. She looked that way whatever he showed her. It must be the sheltered life she'd led. She hadn't even flown in a plane until he brought her here. He had a feeling she'd never tire of seeing new things, having new experiences. And he'd never tire of showing them to her.

He didn't know why he'd never taken her on business trips before. He'd always thought he didn't need her. She was always available on the other end of the telephone if anything came up no matter what time of day it was in California. Now he realized what she'd missed. What he'd missed by not having her with him. He'd missed her insight and her enthusiasm.

He'd also missed seeing things through her eyes. She was sensitive and intuitive. He knew that—he just didn't know what a difference it would make to his viewpoint. On the other hand, with her here, he wasn't even thinking about the merger. It wasn't her fault, and yet maybe it was. She was the one who'd come up with the new ideas. Sometimes he wondered if he even cared. It had seemed so important less than a week ago. Now, what did it matter?

He took her to the stables, which were behind the main house in a grove of trees. Sighting their master, a half dozen proud Arabians, some white, some gray, two bays and a magnificent chestnut whinnied loudly and came racing to the fence.

"Oh, Sam," Claudia said, leaning against the fence. "They're beautiful. They know you, don't they? They're glad to see you."

"Of course they know me," he said, reaching out to stroke their purebred wedge-shaped heads one at a time. "Claudia meet Jaden, El Moktar, Thunder, Pasha, Ranger and Araf."

"Can I pet them?" she asked.

"Go ahead. They'll appreciate it. And give them a lump of sugar." He slipped the sugar into her hand. "These Arabians are bred for intelligence, speed and endurance, but I wouldn't have a horse that didn't have a good disposition. They're one of the few breeds so good-natured that the U.S. Equestrian Federation allows children to exhibit. Do you ride?"

"I took lessons when I was a child. There are stables in the park in San Francisco. I'm afraid it was quite tame, always on the trail, always with an instructor. Afterward we had to brush the horses, feed them and give them water. But they were nothing like these stunning creatures."

Sam grinned. He was as pleased with the compliments as if she'd complimented members of his family. In a way, the horses were just that.

"I chose these horses, I bred them. I'm as proud

of them as if they were my own children, which is a good thing, since I probably won't have any children," he said ruefully.

"That would disappoint your father, wouldn't it?" she asked, holding out her hand to give one of the horses his sugar.

"Let Amina provide the grandchildren," he said, reaching into his pocket for a carrot for his favorite mount. "He'll have to make do."

"Because of Zahara breaking off with you?" she asked, leaning forward to rub her hand on the horse's head.

"Because I'm not the marrying type," he said. "You know me well enough to know that."

"I don't necessarily agree with you," she said after a moment.

He turned to look at her, wondering if she was serious. Curious to see what her viewpoint was.

"I think you could make some woman very happy. Whether she would make you happy is another matter."

"You *do* know me, maybe better than anyone. You can bet my family continues to think I'm too selfish and self-centered to ever marry. Especially after this latest fiasco."

"Am I right in assuming you are not broken-hearted?"

"How can I be brokenhearted if I have no heart? Or so says my sister."

"I think you keep your heart hidden."

"Hmm. If I do, it's for the best, wouldn't you say? Otherwise with a fiancée breaking up with me this way my ego would surely be damaged. Enough about me. What made your marriage fail?"

"I'd rather not talk about it," she said stiffly.

"In other words, it's none of my business," he said. He didn't know what made him suddenly so curious. He'd known she was divorced. He'd never given it much of a thought before. "Let's go for a ride."

"I...I don't know if I'm up to it. I'm really not much of a rider."

"I think Thunder would be just right for you. He's strong but gentle. Arabians are sometimes called hot-blooded, which means spirited and bred for speed, but they're also sensitive and intelligent. We call Thunder the great communicator, since he seems more attuned to his rider than the others. I'll have him saddled up for you."

"If you're sure I can do it," she said.

"Absolutely." Sam wasn't completely sure she'd like riding, but he knew Thunder and he knew he was the best choice for a beginner. He called to one of the stable boys who saddled both Thunder and Sam's favorite Jaden.

Claudia put one foot in his outstretched hand and he boosted her up so she could reach the stirrups. With his hand on her firm hip she swung gracefully over the horse's broad back. When he looked up and met her gaze, he felt a shaft of desire hit him like a bolt of lightning. Desire for his assistant? Impossible. What was wrong with him today? It must be the oasis.

He took a step backward. The oasis or he was having a reaction from his thwarted engagement. Although he'd never felt a single flicker of attraction toward Zahara, who was a beauty by any standard.

And yet he was standing there staring up at Claudia on her horse wondering what was happening. Wondering how he had been so unaware of how her eyes sparkled when she was excited. And how had he not noticed her very attractive body all this time. She was small and compact with a shape that was full and ripe combined with a manner that was unassuming and modest in the extreme. She seemed totally unaware of how she looked whether in his sister's cocktail dress or the casual shirt and pants she was wearing now. If she wasn't aware of her attraction to men, then how could he have been? But something had changed. It was her or him. Or maybe both of them.

While he stood there consumed with contradictory thoughts and feelings and questions that had no answers, she finally broke the eye contact and began talking softly to the horse and rubbing him behind the ears. Almost as if Sam wasn't there. As if she knew what to do because she'd been riding all her life.

He mounted Jaden and they did a slow trot out the back gate into the palm grove, riding slowly between the trees. Sam went first and turned in his saddle to keep an eye on Claudia. There was nothing like being on his horse to make him feel as if he'd really come home. He hadn't realized how much he missed the communication he had with this animal. How much less complicated it was than communicating with a person. Thank God for Zahara falling in love with someone else. Otherwise where would he be now? Stuck in an engagement to please everyone but himself.

How did he ever think he would communicate with a woman he hadn't seen for twenty years? It was ridiculous. He didn't want to contemplate the consequences of a marriage to a stranger.

He was glad they'd come here to the Palmerie.

What a perfect place to leave the world behind and concentrate on the basics of life. Horses, trees, water and family. And then there was Claudia. Claudia who knew exactly where she belonged and it certainly wasn't here.

They left the palmerie and Sam led the way to the dunes on the other side of the compound. The horses dug their hooves into the sand and climbed to the top.

"Are you okay?" Sam called to Claudia. He was glad to see Thunder slow down to take the sand dunes a step at a time instead of racing up and down like a more hotheaded animal would have done. He must know he had a novice rider on his back. Otherwise he would have raced Jaden and Sam to the top.

"So far, yes," she called.

Sam waited until she caught up with him.

"Go on," she said. "You want to run. I'll wait here."

He hesitated then he nodded and gave his horse the command. They took off. The sand blew in his face, the hot wind tore at his clothes and he forgot everything but the feeling of power and strength. When he returned to where Claudia was waiting, the sweat poured off his face, but he couldn't help grinning.

She grinned back. "You're a natural. But you've been riding all your life haven't you?"

"Yes, but it's been a long while since I've been here. Too long. I forgot what it feels like. Next time we'll get you and Thunder running, too."

They cantered slowly back to the house and left the horses with the groom at the stable.

He felt more alive than he had in months. Every muscle felt used. He reached up to help Claudia down from her horse. She slid effortlessly into his arms as if she belonged there. She looked at him, questions in her eyes that he couldn't answer. She licked her lips and there it was again, desire, white and hot and unexpected. He bent down and kissed her and the world spun around. Her lips were soft and sweet and he wanted to kiss her again and again. He heard her gasp with surprise.

"I'm sorry," he said, stepping backward. "Forgive me. I don't know what got into me. It must be this place. Or something else." He looked around as if he wasn't sure where he was. "That was a mistake."

She nodded, then she left the stable so fast he wasn't sure what had happened.

Sam showered and changed clothes. He only hoped Claudia understood that the kiss meant nothing. Only that she was an attractive woman and he was a frustrated man. That's all. Of course she would. Not only was she attractive, but she was sensible.

He went to the kitchen to confer with the cooks. By dinner everything would be back to normal. They'd talk about business and the kiss would be completely forgotten. If he kept replaying it now, it was just that he had nothing else to focus on.

There in the kitchen he heard the servants say they were having guests to dinner, a Bedouin nomad and his son who were passing through and assumed his father was with them. Which reminded him that his father was intent on buying the prize-winning camel and these men would tell him where, when and how.

Claudia went up to her room to get ready for dinner. Her knees were trembling so much she could barely climb the stairs. She'd never been kissed like that before. She'd dreamed of Sam kissing her, but it was better than any dream. And yet it was about as real as a dream.

She walked around the lovely guest room wondering what she should have done. She'd wanted to throw her arms around him and kiss him back. But he'd pulled back and apologized before she knew what was happening. He was sorry he'd kissed her. He'd made that quite clear. Whereas she wasn't sorry at all. She blinked rapidly to keep from crying.

She stared at the clothes Amina had packed for her wondering what was appropriate to wear for dinner. Fortunately the servant girl who'd unpacked her clothes for her knew. She laid out a long, loose traditional cotton gown with embroidery at the neckline. It was Amina's of course and it was beautiful, cool and comfortable and it fit perfectly.

Amina had thought of everything. Except that her brother would kiss his assistant. No one could have expected that. Claudia was still shaking both inside and out. Even after her shower. She knew it meant nothing, but why did he do it? Probably just a reaction from his broken engagement.

She looked in the mirror. She looked different and she was. She'd been kissed. Her cheeks were pink, her lips were red. Her hair was wild. Without Amina to braid it, she had to let it fall to her shoulders in loose waves.

After she got dressed, she stood on the balcony of the guest room as the sun set over the palm grove. She told herself this was all a beautiful dream and when she woke up she'd be back in her office, wearing a suit and low-heeled shoes.

She'd be answering the phone and writing messages for Sam. He'd treat her like an employee as usual and not a desirable woman. A trusted and valued employee, to be sure, but there was a difference in the way they interacted here. A big difference. If only he hadn't kissed her, she could pretend everything was the same.

She couldn't procrastinate any longer. She walked slowly down the stairs and heard voices.

"Ah, Claudia," Sam said, watching her enter the living room. "Meet our guests."

The guests who both wore turbans and loose robes had come to see his father and while disappointed, agreed to join them at the long table for dinner.

Claudia breathed a sigh of relief. They wouldn't be alone. They wouldn't have to think about the kiss. They'd be distracted. No awkward conversation over dinner where they both tried to pretend nothing had happened. Instead all the attention was on the men with their leathery, weather-beaten faces who described their travels while Sam translated for her.

The first course was tiny kebobs, which were served on small plates with forks, although the guests simply picked them up in their fingers. Next a huge platter of couscous was brought to the table and each person helped himself to the light yellow, saffron-flavored grain.

In between courses, the old man named Azuri shared information about the camel races and camel market to be held in two days across the desert. Claudia watched and listened. Even though she couldn't understand a word and had to wait for Sam's translation, it was fascinating for her to study the dynamics, the facial expressions and the occasional shout of excitement or disbelief from both guests and host.

When Sam heard a prize camel would definitely be on the market, he told Claudia that was the one.

"Father has wanted this camel, Zaru, for a while. He's known to be the fastest camel in the country. Always wins these races. But the owner would never sell. Now Father won't rest until he has bought this camel for himself."

"What will he do with him?" Claudia asked.

"Stable him here and race him whenever he can. Be the object of envy of everyone in the country. Enjoy the pride of ownership. If he could own Zaru nothing else would compare. My engagement, the merger, anything."

A few minutes later, the salad was served and Sam said to Claudia, "I have to go to the market at Wadi Halfa and buy the camel for him."

They left her an out. She didn't have to go.

"Will it be expensive?" she asked.

"It doesn't matter," Sam assured her. "He wants it and that's all there is to it. He's been talking about Zaru for years."

This conversation about camels went on and on and was followed by small cups of strong mint tea and honey pastries.

While the two men were discussing the route they would take when they left later that night, Sam turned to Claudia. "I'll leave tomorrow. There are two ways to get to Wadi Halfa. By Land Rover on a road which is the long way, or by horse which is overland and shorter."

"I can guess which one you'll take."

"What about you?"

Startled, she set her tea cup down. "Me?"

"Don't you want to see some authentic camel races, the market, the Bedouins? Don't you want to sleep in a tent?"

She studied his face, knowing without a doubt the excitement she saw in his eyes had nothing to do with her and everything to do with this trip. The kiss that had rocked her world might as well have never taken place. His forgetting it had ever happened hurt like an ache in her side that would never go away. All his attention was on the trip.

He'd invited her along as a tourist. That was all. She could say no, but she wouldn't do that. Instead she swallowed her disappointment.

"Well, yes," she said, "but…"

"Then it's settled," Sam said. "The servants will go ahead in the Land Rover with the supplies, and you and I will leave tomorrow on horses. It's a beautiful ride. And much more interesting than going on the road. It's only a few hours over the dunes. Whereas the car has to go around the mountains on a track, we can cut through."

"Cut through? A few hours on a horse? I've never ridden that much."

"We'll stop to rest. We'll take plenty of water and food. You'll see the desert as no other foreigners do. Only the nomads. You'll have a chance for some outstanding photographs of ancient rock paintings."

She felt herself swept along by his persuasive description. How could she say no? How could she stay here when all the action was happening somewhere else? No use worrying about a repetition of that kiss. She would forget it just as he had. There would be so much going on, it would be just the distraction she needed.

How could she choose to go by Land Rover when he was going on horseback? It was just as it always was. Sam was able to convince her and just about anyone else to do just what he wanted whether they had objections or were the least bit hesitant. Except for Zahara. He couldn't convince her to marry him instead of the man she loved. But maybe he hadn't tried very hard.

In this case, of course she wanted to gallop over the dunes with him at her side. Of course she wasn't going to say no to the adventure of a lifetime. To play Lawrence of Arabia without the risk of being attacked by unfriendly natives.

Here the natives were all friendly and hospitable. Her only enemy was herself. All she had to do was keep reminding herself that Sam did not invite her along on this trip because he couldn't stand to be separated from her. He invited her because he had the hospitality gene. He'd also had it imparted to him at an early age. He could no more be rude or inconsiderate to a guest than to mistreat a horse.

She had to think of this trip as a travelers' dream and not a lovers' rendezvous. And she had to keep her emotions under wrap. If she couldn't, she ought to stay here or at least go in the Land Rover with the servants. That would be the safe thing to do. The prudent thing to do.

But Claudia wasn't feeling prudent. His enthusiasm was contagious. She was in the desert. She was meeting real nomads. She would see camels race and be sold at market. At the same time she was safe and sound with the only man in the world she'd ever love. It was only her heart that was in danger. Very grave danger.

That night Sam put a duffel bag with her clothes in the Land Rover along with the tent, cooking equipment and sleeping bags, which would be driven to the compound at Wadi Halfa by his father's servants. The next morning the two of them took off, their saddlebags filled with bottles of water, dried fruit and bread.

It was early and the air was cool and fresh. The horses seemed as excited and eager as Claudia. Sam, too, looked better than she could remember. He was tanned, relaxed and smiling and eager to talk about their destination. It was a sure way to avoid saying anything personal. No palm reading. No unnecessary touching. No kissing. Those were the unspoken rules.

Seeing him on horseback, at peace with the world, she didn't know how any woman in her right mind could turn him down. She didn't know how, but she was just glad Zahara had done it. Not for her sake, but for Sam's. He never would have been happy with her and all Claudia really wanted was his happiness. At least that's what she told herself.

Their horses walked slowly side by side as Sam explained that Wadi Halfa was under the jurisdiction of a sheikh who would host the event.

"We'll sleep in our own tent, but we'll be his guests."

"And if you buy the camel?"

"I will buy the camel or else die trying," he said. "In which case the sellers will deliver him to my father. But we're not the only one who wants Zaru. He's famous. We may have a fight on our hands." Her concern must have shown on her face, because he reached out to pat her on the shoulder. The kind of friendly gesture you'd give to a colleague or an underling. She was neither. When Sam was around, she didn't know who she was.

"Don't worry, we'll get him. You brought your camera, didn't you? You can show Father the pictures of his new camel winning the race, which he most certainly will do."

Claudia nodded. It was the part about sleeping in the tent that worried her. He said tent and not tents. He couldn't possibly mean they'd be sharing a tent, could he? She didn't have time to worry because a few moments later they were galloping across the dunes.

It was exhilarating with the warm wind tearing at her hair and clothes. Exhilarating but tiring, too. Her hips were sore from bouncing up and down in the saddle and her face was burning. Her hair had come loose and the perspiration was pouring down her temples.

After the dunes Sam turned down some narrow trails through rocky ravines. Fortunately Thunder was remarkably sure-footed and didn't miss a step.

Sam stopped by a spring and dismounted. "Let's take a break," he said, reaching up to help her down. She was so tired she slid off the horse and brushed against Sam's chest as she landed. Oh, no, not again.

Up close she could see herself reflected in his sun goggles and notice the faint creases at the corners of his mouth. He put his hands on her hips to steady her but even when she landed safely he didn't take them away for a long moment. Which was lucky because she was shaking all over, either from the ride or from the close contact with Sam.

Behind his glasses she thought she saw some emotion flicker in his eyes. He leaned forward. She held her breath. Waiting. Wondering. Would he kiss her again? Would she kiss him back this time? Her lips tingled. Only a few inches remained between them.

He lifted his hand and tucked a strand of hair behind her ear. His touch left a trail of sparks on her skin. Then he dropped his hand as if he'd been burned and the moment passed as quickly as it had arrived. It was just as well. They both remembered what had happened the last time she'd dismounted and neither wanted it to happen again.

They sat on rocks and drank from the cool, fresh spring water, splashing it on their faces as well.

"How do you feel?" he asked.

"Okay. Well, maybe a little sore." She didn't realize how much her bottom hurt until she rested against the warm rock. "I've never ridden this much or this far before."

"We're over halfway there," he said. "You're doing fine."

His encouraging smile and words almost made her forget the pain in her backside. She pulled her hair back and tied it up to get it off her neck. She ate a few crackers and an orange from her saddlebag and then they were off again.

In the distance they saw a camel train headed in the same direction as they were. Sam slowed his horse and pulled up next to her.

"They're probably going to the market as we

are," he said. "Many rulers have tried to force the nomads to change their ways, to move to town and to speak our language instead of their own."

"But in some ways, they have changed. Didn't your guests last night travel in a four-by-four?" she asked. "They weren't riding camels."

"You're right. That's one way some have welcomed change. Others regret the old days when they had complete control of the desert. Only they knew where the water sources were. They protected the caravans and raided caravans that didn't pay up. When the first Europeans saw them they were impressed by the romantic lifestyle. They painted pictures of the Bedouin on his camel with his sword at his side. Then and now what's really important to them is to be who they are and control their own destiny."

"I'd say that's what's important to all of us," she said.

He nodded thoughtfully. "Trust you to come up with a universal truth," he said with a smile. Was it her imagination or was Sam smiling more these days? It must be the change of scene. The vacation from the office. If he was worried about his father, the merger or anything else, he concealed it well.

"Which reminds me, I promised to show you

the cave paintings. I'm afraid we've passed them now—we'll have to do it on the way back."

As they got close to Wadi Halfa the sounds of traditional music from stringed instruments came drifting across the sand. Banners swung in the wind. Men dressed in turbans and shimmering veils came riding out to greet them.

They'd arrived and just in time. When Claudia got off her horse, she could barely stand.

When she winced, Sam turned to her with a worried look. "What's wrong?" he asked.

"Nothing, just a little sore."

"I brought some salve, just in case. It works miracles. First we must greet our host."

The host was an imposing figure, well over six feet tall, he was covered in a white robe with the traditional headdress.

"Welcome," he said. "Come and have a cool drink and rest from your trip. I know why you've come," he said, a smile creasing his leathery face.

CHAPTER EIGHT

CLAUDIA didn't need to worry about the sleeping arrangements. The servants who'd gone ahead in the Land Rover had set up two tents for them and her suitcase was there along with a cot made up with sheets of the best Egyptian cotton, and hand-knotted carpets covering the dirt floor. They'd filled a pitcher with cool fresh water and Claudia washed her face and tried to forget how sore she was.

They'd already spent a half hour sitting in the sheikh's tent on a pillow on the ground while drinking tea and eating olives. All the while she'd shifted her weight back and forth on the pillow but nothing could relieve the pain she felt where her bottom hit the saddle. Claudia managed to smile and hopefully say the right things, but it wasn't easy.

She changed out of her dusty travel clothes

and flopped down on the cot on her stomach. Riding across the desert was thrilling but exhausting and she didn't want to move for a long long time. Or get back on a horse for a long time, either. Just then Sam pulled the flap to her tent open and peered inside.

"Ready?" he asked. "You don't look ready."

"Just resting for a minute," she said, staying where she was. "Ready for what? Not another ride just yet."

Sam stepped inside her tent. "No, but it's the first race of the day. You'll get a chance to see Zaru in action."

"Will he win?"

"I almost hope not. It will just cause more attention, have more people bidding on him. Make the price go up. On the other hand…"

"You'll be rooting for him, I'm sure."

Sam walked to the cot and stood over her. "Sure you're okay?"

"How could I not be?" She sat up and gestured at the interior of the tent. "All the comforts of home."

"Except for showers and bathrooms, which are a short walk across the compound as you saw."

"If this is the way Bedouins live, I can see why they don't want to give it up."

"I'm afraid most nomads don't live this way. But it's the sheikh's responsibility to make his guests feel welcome. And it's my responsibility to make sure you don't suffer from that long ride. How do you feel really?"

Claudia debated whether to insist she was fine, but he must have seen something in her expression, because he brought out a small jar from his pocket. "I know you, Claudia, and I can tell by the look on your face you're hurting. It's understandable and this is the magic emulsion guaranteed to make pain disappear."

She held out her hand for the jar, but he told her to turn around and get back down on the cot. She tugged at her pants just an inch or two below her waist and Sam sat on the edge of the cot. *I know you Claudia, and I know you're hurting,* he'd said. As long as he didn't know she was hurting on the inside as well.

"Bruises. They look terrible," he said. "You must be in pain and this is no time for modesty. I'm going to apply this cream and you'll see, you'll feel a lot better." With that he edged her cargo pants further down and she buried her flaming face in the cool sheets.

His strong fingers rubbed the lotion in and produced a kind of warming, cooling, stinging and soothing feeling all at once. She sighed, wishing he'd never stop.

"Amazing," she murmured into the pillow as she felt the potion do its work. "You're a genius."

"It's not me, it's the cream."

He could say it wasn't him, but it was. It might be a miracle cream, but she could tell he had a magic touch.

"What is it?" she mumbled, feeling like she could dissolve into a pool of ecstasy. The touch of his hands on her lower back and the curve of her hips was nothing short of erotic, but that was because of Sam. Any time he touched her, whether deliberately or accidentally she lost her balance, forgot to breathe and felt like she might faint.

"It was made originally for horses."

She swiveled her head to look at him. "Horses? And you're using it on me?"

He grinned at her surprise. "Don't worry. You're not the only filly I've used it on. I wouldn't treat you as a guinea pig. "I've used it myself. And on others."

Claudia wondered what others he'd used it on.

The races took up the rest of the day. The excitement in the air was contagious. Hooves pounded the sand and the air was full of screams and shouts. As expected, Zaru won the race and everyone was talking about him. Still, Sam didn't seem that worried about his price going up. In fact he was as proud of the camel as if he'd already bought him for his father. Claudia took pictures of Sam posing with Zaru after the race.

Someday she would look at these pictures just to assure herself it wasn't all a dream. She'd really been to this exotic place. She'd really camped with Bedouins and ridden a horse across the sand. She'd really seen Sam stand next to a prize-winning camel with his white shirt hanging open showing his gorgeous bronzed chest, his smile a flash of white teeth. He'd read her palm and he'd kissed her.

Yes, these were memories she'd treasure forever. If she looked different from her former self wearing someone else's clothes and her hair loose and untamed, he was just as different from the man who wore a shirt, tie and suit every day to the office.

The camel market was to be the next day. The rest of the day was spent socializing and examining the camels for sale as well as prized horses. Claudia followed Sam around and he introduced her to old and new friends. He translated much of the conversations, but not all, and she wondered what they thought about her. Did they understand why he'd brought her along with him? Sure, she might be his assistant in America, but they must wonder what use she could possibly be at a camel market. She wondered herself.

"You really don't need me here," she said to Sam. "But I'm glad I came. It's fascinating."

"I thought you'd like it," he said. "And I do need you here to cheer on Zaru with me. How else would he have won the race?"

"Is it true camels are normally bad tempered?"

"Like people, some are," he said. "Let's go look at Zaru up close." After asking around they learned where the prize camel was staying with his owners.

There he was, chewing contentedly from a bucket of oats, obviously enjoying the honor accorded to a winner.

After Sam spoke to the owner, he reported to Claudia. "He says Zaru is good-tempered, patient and intelligent. You won't find him kicking or spitting. In fact he says camels don't deserve their bad reputation. Zaru is worth every penny the new owner pays for him. He's a purebred with all kinds of papers and he should live forty years or more. The owner says you can have a ride on him. See for yourself."

"He's quite a salesman, isn't he?" Claudia asked. "I'd love to ride, but…"

"Just around the circle."

She hesitated. She didn't want to add to her pain, but when else would she have a chance to ride any camel, let alone this prize-winning beast.

"Maybe, but I take his picture first, if it's okay."

She got permission and this time she got up close to capture the camel's soft, doelike expression and his long double row of curly eyelashes. Sure enough, he merely gazed calmly at Claudia without a thought of spitting or kicking her.

"I think he likes you," Sam said with a grin.

"Or maybe he's just basking in his fame."

The owner, thinking Claudia had accepted the offer, had the camel go down on his knees so she could mount.

She exchanged a long look with Sam. Would he think her a coward if she didn't go? Might she always regret it if she missed this opportunity?

He gave her a thumbs-up sign and she had no choice. He expected her to take chances. He wanted her to experience it all. She couldn't let him down. With Sam in his country she was a different person from the assistant back home. A braver person. A person who took chances. Who wore different clothes and almost kissed her boss back when he kissed her.

She walked up and spoke a few soft words to

Zaru, then threw one leg over his back and he rose
to his feet slowly making soft moaning sounds.

"Am I too heavy?" she asked Sam, flinging her
arms around the camel's neck.

"Don't worry. It doesn't mean anything. The
moaning is just like the grunting and growling of
a weight-lifter."

When she was up on the camel's back, high in
the air, the owner led them slowly around the
compound. The rocking motion was soothing and
didn't seem to make her bottom any sorer than it
already was.

A few minutes later Sam took her picture with
her camera, the camel kneeled down, she got off
and thanked the owner profusely.

Sam told him he'd see him tomorrow. Both
knew there would be delicate negotiations over
the price of the camel. Claudia wondered how
much Sam was willing to pay.

"Maybe we shouldn't have admired Zaru so
much, so openly," she said as they walked away.
"In terms of driving a bargain."

Sam agreed. "We may have made the price go
up."

"Maybe that was our mistake in the negotiations
with the Bayadhis. We were too eager for the
merger. Maybe we should have played hard to get."

Sam nodded slowly. "Exactly what I told Father. You and I are on the same wavelength as usual. Let's be sure to use the strategy to our advantage. For now, we're only dealing with a camel. Given his reputation, he'll be a costly addition to Father's stable no matter what. And it was worth it to see you ride him. You looked quite at home up there. Are you sure you didn't take camel-riding lessons in the park, too?" he teased.

"Actually camels might be easier than horses to ride," she said. "It almost felt like riding a rocking horse. No bouncing, no jarring."

"They're called the ships of the desert for that very reason, they sway and pitch like a ship."

Maybe that's why her bottom wasn't any worse for wear. She hadn't been riding a camel, she'd been on a ship of the desert.

An hour later dinner was served under an open-air tent. Servants passed trays of lamb that had been roasted on a spit and filled the air with a mouth-watering smell. Claudia and Sam joined the other guests and sat cross-legged on goat-hair carpets while served by women in multicolored, long dresses, their hands decorated with henna dye.

The next course was *Fatoush* salad, made of pita chips, tomatoes, cucumber, onion and parsley and flavored with lemon, which made a cool and refreshing accompaniment to the succulent lamb. The flat bread they called *nan* was hot and crisp straight out of a stone oven and spiced with sumac. All the food was washed down with icy soft drinks.

Children chased each other through the encampment, laughing and shouting. Between courses guests got up and greeted friends. Sam introduced her to at least a dozen men, some in traditional dress, some in casual European clothes.

"Do you know all these people?" she asked.

"I do now. Some are friends of my father. They're all asking about him. Wondering how he is. Asking why he isn't here, too. But the real reason they're stopping by is to ask who you are." He cocked his head to one side and narrowed his eyes as if he wasn't too sure who she was.

"I suppose it's unusual to travel with your assistant from the States."

"So unusual they don't believe me," he said.

"Really?"

"They naturally assume you're my wife. They congratulate me on making such a good choice." He grinned at her.

Claudia's face reddened. "Of course you told them how you feel about marriage."

"If I did, they'd be shocked. They'd treat me like a mental patient. They'd ask why."

"What would you tell them?"

"Just what I tell you. I don't want to share my life with anyone. I'd make a terrible husband. I'd be just like my father, always at work. Always at the office. Only I'd feel guilty, which my father never did. Do you know I hardly ever saw him during my childhood? He was always traveling, always socializing with business people or relatives. He assumed my mother would take care of us, which she did. But why bother getting married and having children if you don't have to and now I don't have to. Zahara has done me a huge favor. I agreed to marry her, showing how accommodating I am and now I don't have to. Can you imagine how relieved and happy I am?"

Claudia nodded. Relieved. He'd said it again. Either he was trying to convince himself or her. Or he really was.

"In order to stop the questions," he continued, "it might be easier if we just pretended to be married. But then I'd have to sleep in your tent. You wouldn't want that, would you?"

Claudia bit her lip. His eyes gleamed with amusement. He was teasing her again and she didn't know how to take it. How would they ever get back to being boss and secretary again?

"And to show your respect you should probably walk five paces behind me. Could you do that?"

"If you like," she said with a demure smile.

"If you were my wife, you wouldn't even be here, you'd probably be at home."

"What would I be doing?"

"Taking care of our eight children. Weaving. Gossiping with the other wives. That's what my mother couldn't take. My father was off at the camel races or christening a new ship. The men had all the fun and she was treated like a concubine and nanny all in one."

"I don't blame her. But surely times have changed?"

"Yes. Quite a bit. Look around. There are plenty of women here. Just as interested in the races and the markets as the men. But it's too late for my parents. They've gone their separate ways."

He sounded like he'd come to terms with his parents' divorce, but Claudia wondered if the hurt still lingered.

The servers came around with small cups of hot, strong coffee and plates of honey pastries. He sipped his coffee, then he asked her a question.

"How would you feel if you had to stay home

and miss all this?" He gestured to the rows of tents, the camels tethered outside, the stable of horses at the edge of the field, and in the distance the shifting sand dunes turning gold in the sunset.

She didn't want to speculate on what she would have done had she been his mother, confined to the home while homesick for her own country. Maybe she would have left, too, once her children were off to school. But if she'd truly been in love…It was hard to imagine. "I'm having a wonderful time. I wouldn't have missed it for the world. I can't believe I'm here."

He gazed at her over his coffee cup, his eyes gleaming with approval. "Good. I thought you'd like it," he said.

"Like it? Riding horseback over the dunes. Eating roasted lamb and watching the camel races. I'll never forget it." She sighed contentedly. "Never."

"Could you live here?" he asked. "Not out here, but in an oasis like Sidi Bou Said?"

Surprised, she set her cup down. He'd asked her a similar question the other night. How could she answer? What could she say? The truth was she'd live anywhere he did. "It's a wonderful vacation spot, but…"

"Don't look so alarmed. It's just a rhetorical question. Of course you couldn't. No one could unless they grew up there. Even then, there are difficulties. Forget I asked you."

"Could you?" she asked.

"I don't know. I've been asking myself. Not that I have to. It's too remote for someone involved in business. Despite the internet access. I guess I sometimes wonder if I have a home and where it is."

There was a long silence. Sam seemed lost in thought, maybe wondering about where he would eventually live and how he would hold out against family expectations.

They got up to leave when two women approached Claudia and pointed to her hands while chattering loudly.

"They want to dye your hands in a pattern like theirs," he said. "Don't worry, it's not permanent. Are you game?"

"Sure, if they want to," she said. Why not go for the whole Bedouin experience?

"They'll take you to their tent and I'll meet you later."

Claudia had the feeling Sam needed some time to himself. He seemed eager to pass her off on the women and she didn't mind going in the least. Soon she'd be back in San Francisco where life was predictable and pleasant, where she was unlikely to meet women in long gowns offering to tattoo her hands or camels racing across the sand.

The women mixed the dark red powder with water and with a tiny stick they painted a pattern on her hands. Then while it dried they served tea and a kind of cookie and sang and danced around the tent. Claudia wished she knew what they were saying when they spoke to her.

Maybe they were asking questions about her just as Sam said. She wanted to tell them this was all business. Sam meant nothing to her. But maybe they wouldn't believe her. Maybe the fortune teller knew more than Claudia thought.

Maybe like Durrah she'd seen more than Claudia wanted her to. Maybe everyone knew how she felt despite all her efforts to act like she didn't care about Sam. As long as everyone didn't include Sam, she didn't care.

Night was falling as she left the women's tent with her hands covered in intricate patterns of dye. She was walking back to her tent when Sam caught up with her.

"Ah," he said, taking her hands in his to examine the work the women had done. "Now you look like you belong."

"They're amazing artists," she said, staring at

his large warm hands holding hers, wishing he'd never let go. But he did.

"It's getting dark," he said. "This is the moment I've been waiting for. It's time for some serious stargazing."

He gathered a large carpet and a bottle of water and they walked a good twenty yards away from the tents and the animals. He spread the carpet out and they lay down flat on their backs. The gas lanterns and the rumble of voices from the compound seemed miles away.

"I don't know if you've ever tried stargazing back in San Francisco or in any big city, but the only thing you can see there with the naked eye are the brightest stars and the moon."

"But if we could see the stars, would they be the same ones we're looking at now?"

"More or less, because we're almost the same latitude, the city light pollution is the reason you can't see much in San Francisco. That's why it's good to get out here, away from it all for many reasons, and see the sky in all its glory."

"Then we won't need a telescope?"

"I'd like to have one someday, but look, there's the Big Dipper and the Little Dipper. The handle of the Little Dipper points to the North Star."

The stars were brilliant in the black sky.

Claudia didn't think she'd ever seen a sight so dramatic.

Sam took her hand in his and pointed the way to the North Star. This time he didn't let go. He kept her hand in his as if it were the most natural thing in the world to lie there under the starry sky holding hands and talking about the stars.

"Makes you feel small and insignificant, doesn't it?" Claudia said breathlessly.

"You feel it, too?" he asked, squeezing her hand.

She tried to say yes but when she opened her mouth no sound came out. It was more happiness than she'd ever expected or wanted. Alone under a desert sky with the man she loved. It didn't matter that he didn't love her or that this moment wouldn't last. She knew that. She also knew enough to live in the moment. To make memories that would last a lifetime.

Sam warmed to his subject, when he found how little Claudia knew about the heavens. He explained how important the constellations were to farmers and nomads.

"For example most farmers know they're supposed to plant in the spring and harvest in the fall, but where the seasons are not well defined like around here, where the weather is pretty much the same year-round, how is anyone supposed to remember when to take the goats to pasture or harvest the dates? The answer is the constellations. Take Scorpius there. Does it look like a scorpion to you?"

"I think so," she said. But she was having a hard time paying attention. Who could blame her when her every nerve ending tingling with the smell of the campfires burning back at the camp, the warm breeze on her face and the scent of sandalwood soap that clung to Sam's clean shirt. Underneath was the carpet and sand. Above were the heavens, unreachable, untouchable and yet, and yet...

"Scorpius is only visible in the summer, so if you were a farmer without a clock or calendar, you could look for him in the night sky and you'd know what to do."

It was a good thing there wasn't going to be a test on Astronomy 101 later, because she was afraid she might forget some of the fine points of his lecture. Oh, she was listening all right, but it was the sound of his voice alone that had the power to distract her and make her want to feel his arms around her, his lips on hers.

"Then there's the North Star," he continued, warming to his subject. "At the handle of the

Little Dipper. Very useful if you're lost out here in the desert."

She murmured something affirmative but all she could think about was what it would be like to honeymoon in a desert tent with only horses, camels and the starry skies above? Of course it would be nice to throw in a few servants, too. The kind who provided cold drinks and hot food and a tent over your head.

"Where were you and Zahara going to honeymoon?" Claudia asked.

"What? I don't think we'd thought that far ahead," Sam said, sounding surprised. "Why do you ask?"

"I was thinking this would be an ideal spot, it's so…beautiful." She almost said "romantic," but stopped herself just in time.

He laughed and let go of her hand. "You don't know Zahara. I don't know her very well, either, and even though she wants to marry the groom, I think her taste would run more to the Ritz in Paris than a tent in the desert. I hope he'll be able to provide for her. As you know, thinking you're in love and actually being in love are two different things."

"I thought you didn't believe in love."

"I don't, but you do."

"Yes," she said softly.

"Even after what you went through?" he asked, turning his head to look at her hoping that his time she might answer and tell him what had happened to her.

She turned to face him. She didn't want to talk about her marriage, but in the dark of the night, under the starry sky, she thought maybe it wouldn't hurt so much.

"I made a mistake," she said. "I married the wrong man. I was young and stupid. He cheated on me with a friend of mine before we were even married, but he confessed and said he'd never do it again. I believed him because I wanted to. I believed it was my friend's fault, so I cut her off, sick at heart she'd do that to me. I had to make a choice, him or her. I chose him."

Her throat clogged with tears and she couldn't speak. The memories came crowding back. The hurt, the anger and the feeling of being betrayed.

"Claudia, I'm sorry. I shouldn't have asked." Sam reached for her hand again and held it against his chest. She could feel his heart pounding.

"No, it's all right," she said, staring up at the sky again to get her bearings just as travelers once did as they crossed the desert.

"Anyway I married him and then it happened

again. A different woman this time. This time I wouldn't listen to him. At least I learned that much. And it was over. All over in a few months. I can't tell you how shocked my parents were. They believe marriage is forever. They blamed me for tossing him out. They thought I ought to forgive him again."

"I don't," Sam said. "You did the right thing."

"I know that, it's just…" Again the tears filled her eyes.

"Don't cry," Sam said, sounding alarmed. He propped himself on his elbow and gently wiped her tears with his handkerchief. "I never should have asked you about it. The man is an idiot. He never deserved you. I can't bear to think of him hurting you like that."

"I'm not hurt anymore," she protested. "I'm fine. In fact I feel better that I told you. You must wonder why I believe in love when you don't. Sometimes I wonder myself," she said, her lips quivering. If it weren't for Sam, maybe she wouldn't. But she knew what she felt for him was completely different from what she had felt for Malcolm.

She sighed a ragged sigh. Time to get back to the stars.

"What's that one up there?" she asked, sitting

up straight. She was determined to get back in the mood by paying more attention.

"Orion the great hunter. He's stalking Taurus the bull and behind him is his dog Canis Major who's chasing Lepus the hare." He sat next to her, put one arm around her shoulders and guided her hand to point to the sky.

The nearness of Sam, the sympathy he felt for her, the warmth of his arm and the side of his body pressed against hers made her tremble all over. She felt like she'd joined the galaxy and was glowing like a star. Surely her face must be radiating as much heat and light as a heavenly body.

It's just an astronomy lesson, she told herself. Along with my true confession. No reason to get so excited. She told herself to stop fantasizing about Sam. Stop pretending this was a romance. He'd listened to her story and she felt better than she had. But this was still a business trip no matter how many confidences they exchanged. He was being kind to her. She understood him and he understood her better.

"Too much for one lesson?" he asked.

The answer was yes, it was too much for one lesson. Too much for one woman who had no experience with real love. She thought she'd been in love once, but she knew now she was wrong. This was a whole different feeling. Sam was unlike any man she'd ever known.

"How did you learn all this?" she asked.

He leaned back on his elbows and let his arm drop from her shoulders. "My sister and I had a tutor once when my father didn't want to send us away to school. Maybe he somehow knew that once we were gone my mother would go, too. Anyway, Marcus taught us everything, math, science and languages. He was an amateur astronomer and he took us out stargazing every night. We thought it was wonderful. But when I tried to look at the sky from my roof deck in San Francisco, it was no where near as clear. So I gave it up. But I haven't forgotten the lessons."

"Oh, look, a shooting star." Claudia tilted her head back. "They're not really stars, are they?"

"They're meteorites, just small pieces of rock. Marcus used to say they were the bonus we got from stargazing. If you stay out for a half hour or more most nights you'll see a shooting star or two. Our tutor was a member of the International Meteor Organization, which made him an official meteor watcher. He was quite passionate about them."

"Like your sister is passionate about clothes

and you're passionate about your horses or the shipping business."

"And you?"

She wrapped her arms around her knees. "That's what your sister asked me. I wish I knew."

Of course she did know she was passionate about Sam, but that was beside the point and this was hardly the time to confess. Never was the time for her to confess that. In fact, there wasn't a good time to ever tell anyone.

If only this astronomy lesson could go on forever. What could be more romantic than the black sky above lit with stars, the soft sand beneath them and Sam listening to her recount her sad marriage after sharing his passion for the heavens with her? It was as close to heaven as she would ever get. Did he feel it, too? Whatever he felt, she understood him better than ever. And she knew better than ever why he would never commit to love and marriage.

"Come on," he said, getting to his feet. "It's time to turn in. It's been a long day."

A long day? It had been an incredible day. It was a day filled with sights and sounds she'd never forget. Sights and sounds made more memorable because she'd shared them with Sam. If only he felt the same about her.

CHAPTER NINE

SAM awoke to the smell of steaming, dark roasted coffee carried in to his tent on a tray by a young man in a long robe and a turban wrapped around his head. He smiled, said good morning in Arabic and left a basket filled with flat bread and dates on a small wicker table.

Sam got up and looked outside. No surprise that it was another warm sunny day in the desert. A perfect day for another camel race. This one would be more important. There would be more competition today. If Zaru won again it would make the price go up for the camel. But how could he not cheer for him? It was almost as if he was theirs already.

Claudia would cheer with him. She seemed to care as much as he did. In the past he'd been with family at these events and they all enjoyed the festivities. But seeing Claudia react was something else. Her dazzling smile, her flushed cheeks and the look in her eyes when she rode that camel were sights he'd never forget.

He had no idea she would be so eager for new experiences, so brave about riding a horse across the desert. How could he? She was his secretary, she sat at a desk and was incredibly efficient and smart. That was all and that was enough. That was all he wanted.

But now? What did he want? Part of him wanted this trip to never end. To continue the discoveries, to find out what else made her eyes light up. What made her able to take chances. How far would she go?

What he knew was that she wore her emotions on her sleeve and he never tired of watching her reactions.

How she'd changed since they'd arrived in this country. Would it have happened to anyone? Surely not. Most women would have avoided being dragged into a family crisis, a broken engagement and a postponed merger. Most women would have gotten on the first plane home instead of attending a camel race. But not Claudia. She looked like there was nothing she'd rather be doing. In fact, she'd said as much.

How many women would want to spend an

evening lying on the sand looking up at the stars listening to him drone on about the constellations, repeating the lessons he'd learned so long ago? He couldn't think of a single one. How many would confess to being betrayed by their husband? He was touched by her confiding in him. He wanted to kill the man who'd made her cry.

Sitting there with his arm around her shoulders showing her stars felt so natural and right, he hoped she felt the same way. How anyone could treat her the way her husband had was beyond belief. He clenched his jaw so tight it locked in place, just thinking of the man who'd cheated on her.

He had no idea if Zahara liked stargazing. It didn't matter anymore. He certainly couldn't picture her on a camel. Couldn't imagine her hair blowing in the wind or getting sunburned like Claudia. Claudia didn't seem to have a vain bone in her body.

Zahara was no longer part of his life and the relief he felt when she'd called off the engagement had only intensified over the past two days. Since she intended to marry the family groom, she must like horses, but he couldn't picture Zahara riding across the desert like Claudia had. The thought of how easily he'd committed to marrying Zahara made him realize how lucky he was to still be free. Free to marry whoever he wanted.

Of course he had no intention of marrying anyone at all. It wouldn't be fair to them. He thought of his mother, back in France, finally living the life she wanted, at home in her own country, speaking her own language, surrounded by friends and family. Her memories of this country were bittersweet. And his father was still bitterly uncomprehending of why she'd left. How could anyone know if marriage would last? There were no guarantees. Not money or common interests, or family ties. Sam was prepared to take risks in business, but not in his personal life.

As he got dressed in a loose white shirt and long cargo shorts he had a feeling today would be just as full of events and maybe a few surprises. He smiled thinking of showing Claudia the souks set up in tents outside this morning. Would she be tempted to buy an amulet, cushions, dresses or earrings? He wanted to buy her something to remember this day, this trip. But he had no idea what she liked.

Strange that he'd known her for two years and yet he couldn't picture her in jewelry or indulging in anything that wasn't practical. In some ways, he felt like he was just getting to know her. Did she just think of him as her boss, someone she had to humor and go along with what he decided? A week ago that would have been fine. But not now. They were more than boss and secretary now. They were friends. He shouldn't have kissed her. But he couldn't help himself.

When he made a knocking sound outside her tent, she called, "Come in."

"Sleep well?" he asked. She looked fresh and wide-awake sitting on the edge of her cot with a coffee cup in her hand. "Don't answer that, I can tell, you are…definitely well rested." He couldn't tell her she looked amazing this morning, so unlike her San Francisco self he couldn't stop staring at her. She'd been changing constantly ever since she arrived in his country and now with her hair damp and in long waves, her eyes gleaming, her skin with a sheen from the desert sun, the transformation was little short of stunning.

Of course he would be stunned. Back in the office, she'd appeared every morning in a suit and sensible shoes, her hair pulled back from her face, ready for a day's work. How could he possibly have imagined there was a beautiful butterfly ready to emerge from the cocoon? No wonder he couldn't stop staring at her.

"I had time for a shower," she said. "I feel great."

"You look great," he said. Great was not the word for it. She looked like a ripe, sun-kissed tropical fruit. It was all he could do to keep from taking her in his arms and kissing her again. He wondered if she'd taste like summer and sunshine.

What was he thinking? One day in the not too distant future they'd be back in the office in San Francisco and all this would be in the past. He couldn't do anything to risk his relationship with Claudia. He couldn't get along without her back there. He must not upset the careful balance they had. They worked so well together. It would be unthinkable to get carried away and do something he'd be sorry for.

He never let his emotions run out of control, as his family knew so well. There should be no problem now. And yet…and yet… No matter what he thought, there was some sort of change going on inside his head. He could blame it on the weather, the sun, the sand or this rapidly changing country he belonged to. Or he could blame it on Claudia.

He had to take care their relationship didn't change just because they were in a different country. The status quo was his goal, but it seemed to be slipping away by the hour.

"But what about your sore bottom? Need another treatment?"

She flushed. "Much better thanks to your magic potion."

"Think you'll ever be able to ride again?"

"Of course. I'm looking forward to it. Now that Thunder and I get on so well. How much longer will we be here?"

"Hopefully we can wrap up the acquisition of the camel by tomorrow. It must be tiring for you living in a tent like this."

"Not at all. It's very comfortable. And what an experience. For you it's nothing, but for me? I'll have something to remember for the rest of my life."

"I'm sure you'll have more than that. Who can say what the future holds?" Who knew indeed? "You'll have all kinds of adventures, get married again. Who knows?"

The idea of Claudia getting married and leaving him gave him pause. He'd never find anyone to take her place. But what could he do? She was a free agent.

She shook her head. "No matter what you read on my palm, I'll never get married again. Now you know why. I'm over it now, but that doesn't mean I'd ever take a chance on love again."

"You'll change your mind," he insisted more to

himself than to her. "You're lovely, smart and clever. Some tall, dark stranger will make you an offer and you won't be able to refuse."

She stood for a moment then sat down again. She looked so surprised, he wondered if he'd never complimented her before?

"And you're still young."

"Almost thirty."

Enough of this disturbing conversation. He wanted to enjoy the day. There wouldn't be many more like this. Eventually they'd have to go back to work. Why was he having so much trouble concentrating on work? He'd been to the desert before. He'd seen camel races. But he'd never been so distracted.

He set his cup down and stood. "Ready? I want to show you the souks. The markets they've set up in tents. You can find anything you want provided you want a camel saddle or a sword or a drum."

"I'll bring some money then."

He shook his head. "Your money isn't good here. If you want something I'll buy it for you. I owe you for coming with me."

Outside the tent she turned to face him. "What do you mean? This is the best vacation I've ever had. I keep pinching myself. I'm in the desert. I rode a horse and a camel. Do you know how amazing that is?"

"I know you didn't want to come."

"Oh." She looked away and a faint blush colored her cheeks. "Did I say that? I was a different person back there. I wouldn't miss this for the world. Someday when I'm old and gray and living somewhere in an apartment in San Francisco I'll have a photo album to remind me of the time I went to the desert."

He tried to picture her being old and gray, but he couldn't. He definitely couldn't picture her growing old alone. Anyone who saw her on vacation, letting down her hair, wearing a ball gown or shorts that exposed her lovely long legs would immediately desire her for their own. If he weren't a sheikh, if he weren't from another part of the world, if he believed in love…

"You'll have more than the photos," he said. "There has to be something out there in the souks that catches your eye." He grabbed her hand. "We'll find you a souvenir or two or three."

They wandered from tent to tent as Claudia tried on agate beads, brass bracelets, tested cushions stuffed with feathers, silver earrings and amulets to ward off evil spirits. She shook a tambourine and tapped on a goatskin drum. She took pictures of the merchants in their stalls and Sam used her camera to take pictures of her wearing a turban and veil.

Sam wanted to buy it all for her, but he restrained himself. He was waiting for the perfect necklace, the best beads and the purest gold, so they kept going, picking up a few small items, bargaining, laughing and talking with the merchants.

A tall merchant with a long white beard held up a beautiful leather bag dyed deep red and decorated with fringe.

"The fringe is not necessary," he explained to them. "It's about decoration, but it's also about movement. When you are riding with this bag hanging from your horse, the fringe is moving. When the wind is blowing your robes are blowing, too. We love beautiful things. We find beauty in movement. We also love power and respect and we try to include these in our craft. Do you understand?" he asked, holding the red bag out so they could see the fringe to advantage.

Claudia nodded and ran her fingers over the soft leather of the bag. Which was all Sam needed to buy that, too. Then he proceeded to buy silver earrings and some rings and a bracelet from the best silversmith.

Claudia tried to protest, but he insisted and when she wore the silver on her arm and her ears and saw it flash in the sunlight, he knew he'd done the right thing. He took more photos of her with the silversmith. These were pictures he had to have.

Of course she must have smiled as his assistant back in the city, but not like this. Or if she had, he hadn't noticed. Not noticed how Claudia's face lighted up when she was happy? What was wrong with him? He was a different person then. So was she.

"I think the desert agrees with you," he said soberly as they strolled past piles of cured leather and silversmiths working in the sun.

"I think so, too," she said, looking around. When she turned her head her earrings flashed in the sun. "The air is so dry, so pure, you can see for miles. Like last night. I'll never forget the view of the stars. Thank you for that. And thank you for listening to my sad story. I don't usually talk about...about what happened. But last night..." Her voice faltered.

"You're welcome," he said, taking her hand in his. When what he really meant was to thank her for trusting him enough to tell him about her past. Thank her for letting him share his passion with her. For letting him buy jewelry for her and for sharing this day with him.

"Let's get something to drink," he said. They ducked into a tent where they sat down at a rough table in the shade to eat juicy chunks of watermelon and drink more mint tea. Juice stained her lips and he couldn't help wondering how she'd taste. When she noticed him staring at her, she looked away. He had no idea what was happening to him. What was clear was that whatever it was had never happened before.

Before they left the souks Claudia confessed she loved the glazed earthenware they served the couscous in but didn't know if she could get it home with her. "And the copper cooking pots. They're beautiful."

"You should have them. We'll buy whatever you want and send it home in the Land Rover."

"I mean all the way home to California."

"We'll pack them up and take them on the plane with us."

What was she thinking? How would she have room for it all in her tiny apartment kitchen? But Sam was so generous she couldn't say no. All she did was mention something she wanted and suddenly it was hers. How could she recreate this atmosphere or this style of cooking back in California?

Maybe she should just enjoy this experience now and realize that soon it would be over. This trip, this place, this feeling of closeness to Sam would be just a memory. She'd have her pictures and her souvenirs, but they just might make her sad knowing that it was all over like a dream.

Still his enthusiasm was contagious and he went overboard buying pots and dishes for her. He hired a young man to carry the goods and on their way out of the souks they passed the spice market. The pungent smell of coriander, cumin and saffron wafted through the air. Before she knew it, Claudia was watching the merchants scoop out the powders into bags and weigh them, then wrap them up for her.

As they loaded everything into the Land Rover, she said "I'll have to get the recipes from your cook at the house, so I'll be able to use these things."

"I didn't know you could cook."

"Of course. Although I've never eaten anything like what I've had since we arrived. At our book club we always have a potluck dinner that's themed to the book we read. For instance when we read *Reading Lolita in Tehran* we all made Persian food. Maybe I'll make a complete dinner with my new spices and pots when we get back." She could make the dinner, but who would come besides her book club or the Knitwits, her knitting club? She couldn't very well ask Sam. After all, he was her boss. Something she was having trouble wrapping her mind around right now.

No matter what had happened here in Tazzatine, when they returned, it would all be the way it was. Every touch of his hand, every smile they'd exchanged, every look between them would be forgotten and they'd be back to normal.

Normal. What a dreadful word. What it meant was early mornings at the office to catch up on the messages that had arrived the night before. Sure, she and Sam would talk, but they'd talk about cargo ships and docking and fees and financial statements. Then there'd be lunches brought in and eaten at her desk, dry sandwiches, nothing like the cumin scented rice or racks of succulent marinated lamb she'd been eating since she got here.

Back to her old office appropriate outfits. No gorgeous borrowed gowns, no handsome men inviting her to go sailing. No bikini worn at a rooftop pool. No exotic nomads living in tents.

Claudia forced herself to smile and not think about the future. "When is the next camel race?" she asked. "We don't want to be late."

A new and larger circular track had been plowed in the sand. Sam pointed out that this was an official race, more important than the one yesterday. Much lower in prestige than the King's Cup in Dubai but if Zaru continued to improve, he might someday race there, too.

"How fast can they run?" she asked.

"Forty miles an hour, or twenty-five miles an hour for an hour. This won't last that long."

"What if Zaru doesn't win?" she asked.

"I almost hope he doesn't, then he won't be so expensive," Sam murmured, looking over his shoulder as if for prospective competitive buyers.

But when the race started he cheered louder than anyone. "Go, Zaru," he shouted.

"Come on, Zaru." Claudia yelled until she was hoarse but Zaru was nowhere near the finish line.

"What's wrong?" Sam said. "Maybe he doesn't have the speed. Maybe Father won't be so keen on my getting him."

"But you said he'd be cheaper if he doesn't win."

"I didn't expect him to come in last," Sam said with a frown.

"Look, he's catching up," Claudia said. She jumped up and down and shouted encouragement. She'd never been to a race of any kind, certainly not a camel race. If she'd known how much fun they were she might have gone to a horse race. Zaru continued to gain. She noticed Sam was just as enthusiastic as she was. He'd grabbed her hand in the excitement and they cheered together.

When Zaru pulled ahead of the pack they were giddy with excitement. Sam grabbed Claudia and kissed her. This time she kissed him back. It took only seconds for both of them to realize it was a big mistake. They'd crossed the line for the second time. If the first time was an accident, what was this?

"Sorry," Sam said, breathing hard. "He won and I got carried away."

"Me, too." Claudia was trying to catch her breath. It was a hot day, the perspiration was dripping off her face and Sam had kissed her. And she'd kissed him. Something she'd wanted to do since forever. She'd felt the kiss down to her toes. He was sorry. He'd gotten carried away. That was all. She couldn't breathe. Couldn't speak. She'd gotten carried away, too. But she wasn't sorry. Not at all.

"Let's go find Zaru," Sam said, running his hand through his hair. If he was affected at all by the kiss, he'd gotten over it fast. He looked pleased, but only because his future camel had won the big race. That was cause for celebration. It was only a brief kiss exchanged between friends. In a few minutes he would have forgotten it. As for Claudia, it would take her a little longer, maybe a lifetime. She couldn't believe she'd actually kissed him back. Had he even noticed? She hoped not.

They met Zaru and his rider and owner in his stall where he was basking in his glory, munching from a bucket of wheat and oats and drinking water.

Claudia didn't understand any of the bargaining, so she just sat on a small leather three-pronged stool and watched and listened as the men talked. She didn't have to understand what Sam was saying. The sound of his voice resonated in her head, caused a vibration deep inside her.

She watched him knowing he wouldn't notice her. He was too intent on making the deal. She'd seen him like this before, but it wasn't about camels, it was about finding a berth for his ship, paying the docking fees or looking for an alternate port or buying a new ship. He was a supreme negotiator. Fair and honest but aggressive, too. As everyone knew, Samir Al-Hamri always got what he wanted.

She knew he was determined to buy the camel

at any cost, and she knew the owner was determined to get the best price so she could imagine how the conversation went even though she didn't understand a single word.

Finally all parties stood and shook hands. They put their arms around each other and kissed on the cheek. Sam told her on the way back to the main tent he was pleased with the deal.

"Then he's yours?" she asked.

"Father's. They'll deliver him next week."

"I didn't see any money change hands."

"No, but we have a bargain. They trust me to pay and I trust they'll deliver the camel."

The rest of the day was spent in traditional dancing, singing and playing music on drums and lute.

For Claudia it was a letdown. She'd been so excited to see Zaru win, then watch Sam succeed in buying the camel she felt drained of energy. Did her letdown have anything to do with that kiss after the race? She refused to consider it. Obviously Sam had forgotten all about it. To him it was a spur-of-the-moment event, a celebration. Nothing to get excited about. Nothing to treasure or remember.

He was more interested in the weather forecast. The wind had picked up and the sand was blowing. The sun was a hazy orange ball in the afternoon sky. She was sitting on a small carpet, a hat pulled down over her ears to keep the sand out of her hair, watching the women dance when Sam came and told her the old-timers were predicting the *simoom*.

"What's that?" she asked, noting a worry line had formed between his eyebrows.

"It's a severe sand storm. The *simoom* can move dunes, obliterate roads and even obscure the sun. Our best bet is to leave now and outrun it. I don't want to be stuck here with only a tent for protection. Are you game or do you want to go in the Land Rover with the servants? You'd definitely be more comfortable."

"How would you get the horses back?"

"I'd ride mine and lead Thunder."

"I'd rather go with you," she said.

"I was hoping you'd say that," he said with an approving smile.

He wanted her to go with him. It wasn't much in the way of compliments, but it was something and at this point, she'd take whatever she could get.

"Change clothes," he said. "Cover up completely, as best you can. Just in case."

He didn't say in case of what, but she'd heard somewhere about a wall of sand that could travel at sixty miles an hour. If she had to be in the middle of a sand storm, she wanted to be with Sam. If she was honest she'd admit she wanted to be with him in the middle of rain, hail, snow or sleet or a warm summer day. She just wanted to be with him.

CHAPTER TEN

"ARE you sure you're ready for another long ride?" Sam asked as the grooms saddled their horses.

She rubbed her hip. "I'm much better, thanks to your magic ointment." And his magic touch, or course, but she didn't mention that. "And I'm used to the horse now."

"Good, because we need to make time."

After thanking their host, saying goodbye to others who were also preparing to leave, they were off across the dunes. Sam turned to look behind them where the sky was dark on the horizon.

"What do you think?" she asked.

"It doesn't look good. I'm glad we left when we did."

Claudia didn't ask any more questions. She concentrated on following Sam as closely as possible, trying not to imagine what would happen if a wall of sand hit them at sixty miles an hour.

She glanced over her shoulder to see the sand spraying up from the ground. No matter how fast they rode it seemed to be after them like a ferocious beast. The sand filled their eyes and ears with grit despite their hats and sand goggles. She tried to call to Sam but the wind blew her words back into her face.

He turned to look at her and wave then he galloped on ahead finally pulling off in a ravine between two boulders. She breathed a sigh of relief to be out of the relentless wind. He helped her down, gave her a drink of water from his carafe.

"Are you okay?" he asked, putting his hands on her shoulders. She couldn't see his eyes behind his glasses. She didn't want to know how worried he was. If he was, and he must be with this kind of storm.

"Yes," she said. But she was tired of fighting the wind and the sand.

"We can't take time to rest, we have to stay ahead of it."

"Is that what we're doing?"

"So far. It could be worse. Much worse. Sorry about missing the cave paintings."

She nodded and got back on her horse. It seemed like days but it was only hours later, long hours of hard riding when they arrived back at the gates of the villa at Sidi Bou Said. When she dismounted, Claudia felt her knees buckle. She'd been straining so hard, trying to keep up, trying to keep the sand out of her eyes and ears that she almost collapsed. "We made it," she muttered. But Sam didn't hear her and this time he didn't catch her when she slid off her horse. He was too busy talking to the grooms.

"They say Father wants me to call him right away," he said. "Something's up. I'll have a quick shower and call him." He tilted her chin with his thumb and surveyed her face. "You were superb out there. No one could have done better." He traced his index finger along her jawline. She felt the fine grains of sand on her skin. "Get your clothes off. Wash up."

Claudia nodded and went upstairs to have a long shower, his words echoing in her head. *Superb. No one better.* She let the cool water run through her hair and over her body. She scrubbed her skin and washed her hair over and over. It took forever to finally get the sand off every part of her body. Then she toweled off briskly until her skin was prickly.

She found one of Amina's outfits, an all-cotton shirt with matching shorts and sandals and went downstairs. The house was quiet except for the servants who had prepared a cool eggplant and tomato salad with olives and lemon.

They set a table for the two of them on the patio in the arbor under the fig trees. She was famished but she didn't want to eat without Sam. Passing by the office, she heard his voice.

When Sam appeared on the patio his dark eyes were gleaming. His hair was still damp from the shower and he smelled like soap and leather.

"You look better," he said, his gaze taking in her hair, her shirt, shorts and legs. "How do you feel?"

She felt sore, tired yet super-charged at the same time. "What's happened?"

"Father says the Bayadhis are ready to come back to the table. We should head back to the city tomorrow."

"What happened?" she asked eagerly.

"They were intrigued by your idea of considering the benefits of our ships on their contracts. So you get the credit. If it works out."

"There's no guarantee," she said.

"Not yet. But Father is tired of the uncertainty. I'm afraid it's taken a toll on him. Which is why we must get back. He's talking of retiring. Especially when I told him I'd bought the camel. He sees himself as devoting himself to camel-racing. He wants the merger to go through, but he's ready to give up responsibility. He already had too much."

"What does that mean?"

"It means if it goes through I'd have much more to do. Both here and around the globe. I'd be taking over his job as well as my own and who knows what else."

"Would you be based here in Tazzatine?" she asked, trying to conceal the fear that threatened to tear her whole world apart. Sam gone. Sam in Tazzatine. Claudia a world away. She knew he could never be hers. All she asked was to see him every day.

"Probably. At least part of the time."

"You don't seem upset."

"I'm not that surprised. I knew it would happen sooner or later. This is sooner, but I understand why he wants to get away from the stress. And maybe I'm ready for a new challenge. Are you?"

"Me? I...I don't know."

"You'll have a bigger job, more money, more perks."

She didn't want more money and more perks.

She wanted Sam. It wasn't that unexpected that he would one day take over for his father. But not so soon. Her mind was spinning.

"But if the merger doesn't go through…"

He shrugged. "Then Father will have to keep the office going here and I'll come back to California. But I trust you to come up with a solution."

"I'll try," she said.

"If anyone can bring the two sides together, you can. Father will have to agree if he wants this deal to work. We'll leave first thing in the morning." Sam gave her an encouraging smile. He had faith in her. He thought she was smart and perceptive. She appreciated that. She only wished he found her desirable as well. She might as well wish the skies would shower her with meteors every night.

They sat down at the table and she tried to eat, but her stomach was tied up in knots. The pressure Sam put on her seemed unbearable. He had way too much confidence in her. He thought she could run the office in California. He thought she could talk the Bayadhis into agreeing to the merger.

While she sipped her iced tea, he piled a mound of salad on their plates, but then he, too, seemed to lose his appetite.

She tried to eat, but the food seemed to stick in her throat. She tried not the think of the decision that was hanging over her like a wrecker's ball and the delicate negotiations ahead.

Sam acted like nothing had happened. Instead of eating, he talked animatedly about Amina and the family news he'd received from his father. Everything but what was most important. Maybe he thought he was keeping her from worrying. Instead she worried even more. How could she make the merger take place if the families were too far apart?

Why should she try? It would be best for her if it all fell apart. She could arrange it so it looked like she was trying, but leave a loophole that the Bayadhis were sure to notice. It would end the merger and she would get Sam back. But she knew she couldn't let him and his family down. And she couldn't quit her job. Not yet.

Sam watched Claudia out of the corner of his eye while he ate his salad. He knew he'd given her a big job. He also knew she was up to it. He needed her as he never had before. He had no choice. If the merger didn't go through it would be a failure for the family business. His father would take it personally. If it did go through, he'd have a big job. So would Claudia. He'd have to be here and everywhere else, too. He couldn't do it without Claudia working for him in an office across the world.

She was ideal for the job of running the San Francisco office. She knew more than she thought she did. She was better at some things than he was. He'd miss her. He'd miss his right-hand woman and he'd miss the companion of these last few days, the other Claudia. The one who'd worn a bikini at the pool, the one who'd braved the sandstorm because he told her they could make it. The one he'd kissed and who'd kissed him back. But there was no way he could have them both.

He couldn't forget the kiss. He didn't know why. She didn't mean to kiss him any more than he'd meant to kiss her. The first time was a mistake, the second time was because he couldn't help himself.

Why couldn't he get over it? He'd kissed dozens of women and yet he couldn't remember a single kiss or even the names of the women. Maybe it was just that it was so unexpected. He couldn't be in love. According to Claudia love made you lose your appetite and your concentration. All right, so he hadn't been eating or sleeping well or thinking well, either. But that didn't mean anything.

If he'd fallen in love with Claudia it would be inconvenient to say the least. And where would they live? He'd asked her twice if she could imagine herself living here. She'd said no. He was not going to repeat his father's mistake and bring a bride to be homesick and lonely here or anywhere.

Claudia had kissed him. That much he knew for sure. He couldn't believe it really happened. But it had and he had to deal with it. He was an expert at dealing with things that didn't fit into the norm. Everyone who knew him knew he was pragmatic and adaptable. But that kiss was not like anything else that had happened to him and he hadn't adapted to it yet.

He also couldn't reconcile the two sides of her. He didn't know who she really was. Maybe she didn't, either. He just knew she had to say yes to his plan. It made perfect sense. There was no one else he'd trust to run the office. This way he'd get to see her sometimes. He'd fly in for a meeting in San Francisco, they'd talk, have lunch and he'd be off. Just like old times. Only not at all like old times.

Maybe if he kissed her again he could get it out of his mind. He'd realize a kiss is just a kiss. On the other hand, if he wasn't in love, he must have some strange disease. Not only could he not eat or sleep, he couldn't concentrate on anything except for Claudia. These were symptoms he wouldn't want to share with any doctor. He'd just laugh and tell·him what he didn't want to hear. He was in love.

"I have an idea," she said suddenly, interrupting his thoughts. "I need to look something up on the Internet."

He put his fork down. "Go ahead. I've got some calls to make."

She nodded, her gaze fastened on something in the distance. "I'm not sure I can find it, but if I do…It's just something I read somewhere."

Claudia was up half the night. They didn't talk until the next morning. He stopped by the office to offer his services, but she said she needed to be alone and work something out.

"What did you find?" he asked.

"A new maritime law the European Union has just passed. It might help us. I need to do some more research, and make some calls when we get back to your office. Don't tell your father yet."

"I won't, but I know you. You wouldn't say anything unless you were pretty sure."

He grinned at her and her heart skipped a beat.

"Sam, if this works and the merger goes through…"

"I know what you're going to say."

She swallowed hard. "You do?"

"You're going to ask for a raise and a vacation. Ask me—you can have anything you want." He leaned forward and cupped her chin in his hand. Then he very slowly kissed her on the lips. His lips were warm and sure. She put her arms around him and kissed him back. He moaned and held her close.

"Claudia," he said, pulling back to look into her eyes. "What will I do without you?"

Speechless, she shook her head.

He kissed her again. She couldn't have backed away, she could have protested, but she didn't.

She knew she'd regret it. She knew she should keep her distance, but she wasn't made of stone. Soon she'd be gone from this magic place and this would all be a memory. Nothing more. Was it so wrong to take whatever she could get now?

He said she could have anything she wanted. Anything but him. She couldn't tell him now she was leaving. He was too happy. Too hopeful.

On the return drive, they held hands and Claudia watched the scenery go by knowing she'd never see it again. Her head was full of conflicting thoughts. The challenge of making the merger work, and if it did, the reality of losing everything she wanted. Her job and Sam. Not that he'd fire her, he'd promote her, but she'd have to quit. It was clear. She couldn't work for him anymore.

The two families met the next day. The air in the Al-Hamri office was cool, almost frigid and so was the atmosphere at first. The Bayadhi family sat on one side of the table, the Al-Hamris with Claudia on the other. Each side was prepared to get what they wanted or walk away from the table.

Claudia was dressed in new clothes furnished by Amina from her boutique: a slim linen skirt and matching jacket. Her bare legs were tanned and she wore leopard print ballet flats. She felt like a different person than the woman who'd stepped off the plane only two weeks ago. The admiring look Sam gave her told her he thought so, too.

She studied the faces across the table. The old man who'd been Sam's father's rival all these years and three of his children, who would run the company someday, maybe even today. But what company? The new merged company or the old one they were hanging onto?

Sam had greeted everyone warmly. She always admired how cool he was under pressure. He claimed he wasn't worried. That he didn't feel any pressure.

"I know you and I know you have everything under control," he'd said before the meeting. He put his hands on her shoulders and looked into her eyes, a smile tugging the corners of his mouth. She summoned all her willpower and smiled back at him with confidence. This was it. It was in her hands.

If all went well she would save the merger. And she'd say goodbye to Sam. He'd stay here. She'd go back to San Francisco. She'd quit her job. She couldn't take it anymore, loving him and knowing he thought of her as an employee and nothing more.

Or she could withhold her information and let the merger fail and they'd go on as they were. Then at least she'd have Sam from nine-to-five every day and sometimes on the weekends or late at night. Was it better than nothing?

"Ready, Ms. Bradford?" Everyone was looking at her. She opened her briefcase, took out her laptop and motioned for the Bayadhis' lawyer to go first.

He said what she knew he'd say, that merging the two companies would violate a European Union Maritime Law that would prevent them from doing business within the EU.

"I'm sorry, but for obvious reasons, the merger would not do any good for either party," he said and closed his briefcase with a final snap. The Bayadhi family were almost out of their chairs, when Claudia asked for a moment to respond.

Sam's father looked at her expectantly as if to say, now what are you going to do? Sam, however, just kept his dark gaze steady. They'd been through these negotiations before, but she'd never had anything personal at stake before.

It was now or never. Agree with them, and let the merger fail or come up with a solution and let her life change forever. No more job. No more Sam. No more Tazzatine. No more desert or oasis, or horses.

She took a deep breath. "There is a way around this new regulation," she said. "In a similar case two years ago concerning a shipping company which changed its registration from Liberia to Bermuda. In this way bypassing Section 243 of the EU Maritime Code regarding shipping registration. We can do the same because Bermuda has just received a special exemption."

The Bayadhis looked at each other. They asked for time to reconsider. Fifteen minutes. They shook hands and walked out of the room.

"Claudia, that's brilliant," Sam said, clasping her hand in his.

His father sat in his chair for a long moment, before he stood and congratulated her. "Sam was right about you," he said. "You've saved the day. They can't say no now."

"They can," Sam said, "but I don't think they will."

When the Bayadhis came back in the room they were all smiles. Sam's father was right. They couldn't say no. They had no more reason to say no. It was time to celebrate. The Al-Hamris hosted a reception in their office, which Sam had planned, and had ordered fruit drinks and an array of delicious finger food, both savory appetizers like flaky stuffed pastries and little sugared tarts; he was so confident that they would be called for. Several others from both companies joined them and the excited talk was all about expansion, new offices, new routes and new personnel.

"You'll be the one to draw up the new organization chart," Sam said, handing Claudia a glass of sparkling juice as they stood apart from the others at the window looking out at the harbor where an Al-Hamri ship was unloading freight.

Tell him, tell him now, she said to herself. Tell him you'll do the chart but after that, you will be gone. Gone from his office, gone from the company and gone from his life.

"What will you do with the bonus I'm giving you for saving the day? Where will you go on your vacation I'm giving you? Wherever it is, I'll go with you."

She shook her head. "I don't need a bonus, Sam, I was just doing my job. And I've just had the best vacation of my life. I'll never forget this time in your country. I'm just happy it worked out so well. But I ought to get back to San Francisco soon." Her heart fell thinking of facing the city without him there.

"There's no need to rush. We need to celebrate. Really celebrate. I mean to take you sailing and sightseeing here in the city. There's something I want to tell you. Ask your opinion about."

"Ask me now. You've already done enough for me. And I've been gone long enough." Though her lips were trembling, she forced herself to smile politely. It was the only way. He must not guess how she felt.

"I understand," he said. "You're homesick. I should have realized it's not been easy dealing with us foreigners and our strange customs. By all means, you should leave whenever you want to." His voice was suddenly cool and detached. If it was anyone else she would think she'd hurt his feelings. But Sam claimed he didn't have any.

"Tomorrow," she said.

"Tomorrow," he repeated with a frown.

"There's something I have to tell you right now," she said. "I hope you won't take offense."

"Of course not. You couldn't possibly offend me after all we've been through together. Tell me anything."

"Could we go somewhere else?" she asked, glancing over her shoulder at the small groups of smiling employees who represented the new, premier shipping company, all talking excitedly about the plans.

CHAPTER ELEVEN

BEFORE Sam left the party, his father motioned to him and murmured in his ear. "She's a wonderful woman," he said. "Don't let her go."

Sam nodded. "I won't," he said. But how could he make her stay when she didn't want to. This was the twenty-first century. Women all over the world had rights and power. Claudia had more than most. She was smarter than most. More desirable than most. And he wanted her more than he'd ever wanted anything. But she obviously didn't want him. He couldn't blame her. He could only offer her a different life than she knew or wanted. And that never worked. He knew more than he wanted to about that kind of experiment. And Claudia had already told him twice what he didn't want to know.

He led her to the elevator and up to his penthouse apartment. A few moments ago he was on top of the world, he was going to tell Claudia he was in love with her. He was going to ask her to marry him and then he realized how wrong it would be. She'd never last here any more than his mother had.

He had a hollow feeling in the pit of his stomach that his world was going to fall apart. And it wasn't just that he'd skipped breakfast today. Claudia looked like she was going to announce the end of the world.

What did she have to say? Whatever it was it wasn't good.

He flung the doors to the balcony open and the sun streamed in. The view was as spectacular as ever, but he couldn't appreciate the sight of Al-Hamri ships or the blue waters or the winding corniche along the seaside. He rubbed his hands together. Claudia looked so pale he was afraid she was sick.

Alarmed, he said, "Sit down. Are you all right? Are you sick?" He took her hands in his. They were cold. "What's wrong? My God, Claudia, tell me what's wrong?" He couldn't stand to see her suffer. He couldn't stand to lose her.

She snatched her hands back. "Nothing. I'm fine."

She walked around the room as if she didn't

know where she was going. A feeling of despair threatened to overtake him. His desperation was growing by the minute.

"What is it?" he said. "I must know now."

A moment later she stopped pacing and faced him. "I'm leaving, Sam."

"No, don't go yet. Let's talk this over."

"It won't work. I'm leaving the job. I can't work for you anymore."

"You're quitting?" he asked dumbfounded. "What have I done?"

"Nothing. You've been the best boss in the world. But I need to move on. Do something different." She licked her lips. The lips he wanted to kiss.

"You're not happy here, I can understand that." There it was, out in the open. "It's too different. My mother felt the same way."

"I am happy here. I love your country—it's an exciting place to be. It's beautiful and exotic but I can't stay."

"You don't have to stay. You can work wherever you want. We have offices all over the world. But don't leave the company. Don't leave me. I need you. I love you."

She staggered backward and bumped into the leather couch. Now she looked like she was going to faint.

"It's a shock, I know," he said. "I feel shocked myself. It's about time I realized what's been happening to me. I've fallen in love with you." He smiled at her, but she didn't return his smile. He was going to have to do better. She had to believe him. She had to.

"Sam, you can't be in love with me. You don't believe in love."

He grabbed her shoulders and looked into her eyes. What could he say? "I know. I know what I said. But I was wrong. I have all the symptoms, the ones you told me about. I can't eat, I haven't slept for days. And my heart…" He took her hand and placed it on his heart. "Feel that."

"Oh," she said, her eyes wide. "Sam, are you all right?"

"No, I'm not all right. I won't be all right until you tell me you love me and you'll marry me."

"This is all my fault," she said. "Those symptoms I told you about, I didn't realize you'd take them seriously."

He grabbed her hand, and leveled his gaze at her. "Listen to me. You have to hear me out before you turn me down again. I'll tell you how serious I am about you. You've taught me to appreciate my country in a way I never did before. You see the good side of everything and everyone. I've never had such a good time as I've had with you here. I've been working with you for over two years and I thought I knew you. I knew how smart you were, how hardworking and how dedicated, but I never knew how beautiful you were, how you look with your hair wet, or in a sandstorm or in a ball gown. And how you manage to meet every emergency with good humor. You amaze me. You dazzle me. You enchant me." His voice dropped. If she didn't believe him he was lost.

"Sam, stop," she protested, her cheeks bright pink. "You don't need to flatter me."

"It's not flattery if it's the truth. And I need to tell you how I feel about you. Because if I don't...you'll never know. You'll think I'm the same, cold, uncaring boss you always knew."

"I never thought that," she said soberly, blinking back a tear.

"What I'm trying to say," he continued, "is that I don't know when it happened. When I fell in love with you. Maybe it was when you rode across the desert with me, or got up on that camel, or lay on the sand looking at the stars. I resisted. I told myself it wasn't possible. I didn't believe in love, but you know that. I told myself it was a reaction from Zahara's rejection. But I was wrong. It was you. It was always you. It just took me forever to realize it."

"I…I don't know what to say."

"I think I know how you feel. You're afraid of making a commitment. You think because your first marriage didn't work, you don't want to take another chance."

Claudia shook her head. She wanted to believe Sam, but how could she? How could she believe he could have changed so much so fast? She'd been in love with him for two years, and he'd fallen in love with her in a few days. Was that possible? She'd felt his heart pound. "I'm just worried…" she said.

"Of course you're worried. You're worried you'll be homesick like my mother was. I told you we don't have to stay here. We can live anywhere."

"That's not it. I could live here happily. Everyone here has been wonderful to me. Your home in the oasis is a magical place. The capitol city is booming and I'd love to be a part of the boom. I think I've fallen in love with your country."

"But not with me. I understand. I've sprung this on you too soon. Too suddenly."

Claudia choked on a laugh. Suddenly. He

thought he'd come on to her too fast. A sense of wonder and happiness filled her heart. He loved her. He really loved her.

"Sam," she said, putting her hand on his rapidly beating heart again. "I've been in love with you for two years. I don't know when it happened. Maybe it was the night we worked late on the strike at the docks and you drove me home at midnight. Or maybe when you gave me such a glowing recommendation or when I got you out of the charity auction. Or when you brought me flowers on my birthday."

His smile sent sparks shooting in the air. "Then you're over your heartbreak. You're willing to take a chance on love again?"

She nodded and put her hands on his shoulders, returning his smile with her own. Her eyes filled with happy tears and she said, "I love you, Sam. I always have and I always will. I'll marry you and live wherever you want to live." He kissed her then, a deep, thrilling kiss that sealed the promise that their love would last forever.

EPILOGUE

CLAUDIA's wedding day at Sidi Bou Said in the oasis was as perfect as it could be. Teams of chefs had arrived from the capitol the day before and the smell of spices and roasting meats came wafting from the kitchen.

Amina was there in a flowing caftan as her attendant. She was also there to fit Claudia's white wedding dress on her and to style her hair in a way that made her look natural and glamorous at the same time.

"There," Amina said with a satisfied smile as she placed a single white rose in Claudia's hair. "You look beautiful." She stepped back to admire the dress, the hair and her future sister-in-law.

"So the fortune teller was right," Amina said. "There was a man in your future and you found wealth and happiness."

"Yes, I did," Claudia said, her cheeks flushed and her eyes glowing. "I must thank you for your part."

"Don't thank me. I did nothing. It was you. I knew you were right for Sam the minute I saw you."

Claudia went out on the balcony and looked down at the guests assembled in the walled garden. Water cascaded from the fountains. Hydrangeas bloomed against the gate. Servants stood just inside the tall, arched windows, ready for the wedding feast. The musicians were playing traditional songs on the lute and guitar.

Sam was standing at the flower-covered bower looking more handsome than ever in his black tuxedo. As if he felt her eyes on him, he looked up and met her gaze. For a long moment she stood there, feeling the connection between them stronger than a rope of steel. There were people everywhere but for one moment it was only Sam and Claudia alone. They had each other and that was all they needed. The electricity between them fairly sizzled.

Finally Claudia turned and followed Amina down the stairs as the musicians played the wedding march. She walked down a path of cream limestone through a Moorish courtyard on her way to marry the tall, dark, handsome sheikh of her dreams. And after a honeymoon in a tent in the desert, they would live happily ever after. It was guaranteed. The fortune teller said so and she was always right.

MILLS & BOON

Romance

On sale 6th June 2008

*Enjoy a gondola ride along Venice's canals, join
a royal wedding or take a romantic stroll through
London...all this month with Mills & Boon® Romance!*

THE PREGNANCY PROMISE *by Barbara McMahon*

Waiting to hear the pitter patter of tiny feet? Don't miss the
first of the brilliant *Unexpectedly Expecting!* duet. Lianne's
gorgeous boss discovers her wish-list for Mr Right. Can
he admit to secretly desiring a family?

THE ITALIAN'S CINDERELLA BRIDE *by Lucy Gordon*

Despite rejecting the world, Count Pietro can't ignore the
bedraggled waif in his *palazzo*. Will Ruth find comfort
in this proud, damaged Count...?

SAYING YES TO THE MILLIONAIRE *by Fiona Harper*

Second in the spectacular *A Bride for all Seasons*, cautious
Fern spends four days with dreamy Josh. Can she break his rule
of never staying in one place – or with one woman – for long...?

HER ROYAL WEDDING WISH *by Cara Colter*

Princess Shoshauna craves love, not duty. In danger,
Jake must protect her – and she dreams of a royal marriage
to this hardened soldier...

Available at WHSmith, Tesco, ASDA, and all good bookshops
www.millsandboon.co.uk

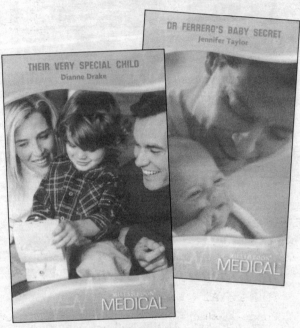

MILLS & BOON®

MEDICAL™

**Pulse-raising romance –
Heart-racing medical drama**

THEIR VERY SPECIAL CHILD
Dianne Drake

DR FERRERO'S BABY SECRET
Jennifer Taylor

MEDICAL

MEDICAL

6 brand-new titles each month

Available on the first Friday of every month
from WHSmith, ASDA, Tesco
and all good bookshops
www.millsandboon.co.uk

GEN/03/RTL11

0508/05a

MILLS & BOON
BY REQUEST
3
NOVELS ONLY
£4.99

**On sale
6th June 2008**

*In June 2008 Mills
& Boon present two
bestselling collections,
each featuring
fabulous romances by
favourite authors...*

The Italian's Convenient Wife

Featuring

The Italian's Suitable Wife by Lucy Monroe
The Italian's Love-Child by Sharon Kendrick
The Italian's Token Wife by Julia James

Available at WHSmith, Tesco, ASDA, and all good bookshops
www.millsandboon.co.uk

0508/05b

**On sale
6th June 2008**

MILLS & BOON
BY REQUEST
3
NOVELS ONLY
£4.99

Don't miss
out on these
fabulous
stories!

Married to a Mistress

Featuring

The Forbidden Mistress by Anne Mather
Mistress to Her Husband by Penny Jordan
The Mistress Wife by Lynne Graham

Available at WHSmith, Tesco, ASDA, and all good bookshops
www.millsandboon.co.uk

Celebrate our centenary year wit
24 special short stories!

ONLY £1.49! EACH

A special 100th Birthday Collection from your favourite authors including:

**Penny Jordan • Diana Palmer • Lucy Gordon
Carole Mortimer • Betty Neels
Debbie Macomber • Sharon Kendrick
Alexandra Sellers • Nicola Cornick**

Two stories published every month from January 2008 to January 2009

Collect all 24 stories to complete the set!

MILLS & BOON
Pure reading pleasure

www.millsandboon.co.uk

Celebrate 100 years of pure reading pleasure with Mills & Boon®

To mark our centenary, each month we're publishing a special 100th Birthday Edition. These celebratory editions are packed with extra features and include a FREE bonus story.

Plus, starting in February you'll have the chance to enter a fabulous monthly prize draw. See 100th Birthday Edition books for details.

Now that's worth celebrating!

15th February 2008

Raintree: Inferno by Linda Howard
Includes FREE bonus story Loving Evangeline
A double dose of Linda Howard's heady mix of passion and adventure

4th April 2008

The Guardian's Forbidden Mistress by Miranda Lee
Includes FREE bonus story The Magnate's Mistress
Two glamorous and sensual reads from favourite author Miranda Lee!

2nd May 2008

The Last Rake in London by Nicola Cornick
Includes FREE bonus story The Notorious Lord
Lose yourself in two tales of high society and rakish seduction!

Look for Mills & Boon 100th Birthday Editions at your favourite bookseller or visit
www.millsandboon.co.uk

0108/CENTENARY_2-IN-1

FREE

4 BOOKS AND A SURPRISE GIFT!

We would like to take this opportunity to thank you for reading this Mills & Boon® book by offering you the chance to take FOUR more specially selected titles from the Romance series absolutely FREE! We're also making this offer to introduce you to the benefits of the Mills & Boon® Reader Service™—

- ★ **FREE home delivery**
- ★ **FREE gifts and competitions**
- ★ **FREE monthly Newsletter**
- ★ **Books available before they're in the shops**
- ★ **Exclusive Reader Service offers**

Accepting these FREE books and gift places you under no obligation to buy; you may cancel at any time, even after receiving your free shipment. Simply complete your details below and return the entire page to the address below. You don't even need a stamp!

YES! Please send me 4 free Romance books and a surprise gift. I understand that unless you hear from me, I will receive 6 superb new titles every month for just £2.99 each, postage and packing free. I am under no obligation to purchase any books and may cancel my subscription at any time. The free books and gift will be mine to keep in any case.

N8ZEE

Ms/Mrs/Miss/Mr..............................Initials ....
BLOCK CAPITALS PLEASE

Surname ....

Address ....

....

....Postcode ....

Send this whole page to:
The Reader Service, FREEPOST CN81, Croydon, CR9 3WZ

Offer valid in UK only and is not available to current Mills & Boon® Reader Service™subscribers to this series. Overseas and Eire please write for details. We reserve the right to refuse an application and applicants must be aged 18 years or over. Only one application per household. Terms and prices subject to change without notice. Offer expires 31st July 2008. As a result of this application, you may receive offers from Harlequin Mills & Boon and other carefully selected companies. If you would prefer not to share in this opportunity please write to The Data Manager at PO Box 676, Richmond, TW9 1WU.

Mills & Boon® is a registered trademark owned by Harlequin Mills & Boon Limited.
The Mills & Boon® Reader Service™ is being used as a trademark.